THE SON OF YORK

THE SON OF YORK

Margaret Abbey

84004

Chivers Press
Bath, Avon, England ● G.K. Hall & Co.
Thorndike, Maine USA

This Large Print edition is published by Chivers Press, England, and by G.K. Hall & Co., USA.

Published in 1995 in the U.K. by arrangement with Robert Hale Limited.

Published in 1995 in the U.S. by arrangement with Robert Hale Limited.

U.K. Hardcover ISBN 0 7451 2555 7 (Chivers Large Print)
U.K. Softcover   ISBN 0 7451 2567 0 (Camden Large Print)
U.S. Softcover   ISBN 0 8161 7498 9 (Nightingale Collection Edition)

The text of this Large Print edition is unabridged.
Other aspects of the book may vary from the original edition.

Set in 16 pt. New Times Roman.

Printed in Great Britain on acid-free paper.

British Library Cataloguing in Publication Data available

Library of Congress Cataloging-in-Publication Data

Abbey, Margaret.
   The son of York/ Margaret Abbey.
     p. cm.
   ISBN 0–8161–7498–9 (lg. print : lsc)
   1. Great Britain—History—House of York, 1461–1485—Fiction.
2. Large type books. I. Title.
[PR6051.B28S66 1995]
823'.914—dc20   94–33761

For
Audrey Strange
A Good Friend and Fellow Ricardian

Messenger from Lord Stanley to William, Lord Hastings.
'He dreamed tonight the boar had razed his helm.'

Tragedy of Richard III, Act 3, Scene 2:
SHAKESPEARE.

AUTHOR'S NOTE

The characters of Beaumont, Langham, Meg Wollatt, Jake Garnet and Bess are fictitious. After considerable reading and research, I feel in agreement with historians who believe Perkin Warbeck to have been Richard Duke of York. Since this is possible, what more likely than Richard would have asked one of his trusted gentlemen to take him to Burgundy for safety?

M. A.

PART ONE

Spring 1479

CHAPTER ONE

The inn seemed a poor place, small and secluded. The tap-room was beginning to empty of customers, though one or two were still lingering over their ale. The stranger paused in the doorway, his eyes passing from the freshly strewn rushes on the floor to the rough but well-polished wood of the table and stools. He had slept in worse places. It must serve. He was too weary to ride further and his horse needed rest.

He walked to the table and called for attention. The yokels put down their leathern jacks to stare at him curiously. The inn wench came at once. She was young, and clean enough. Just now her voice sounded flat, overtired.

'You called, sir?'

He looked up surprised that her tone carried none of the Sussex burr he had expected. She pushed back a damp tendril of her brown hair and stood waiting for his order, patient but unsmiling.

'I wish to stay here for the night. I need a private room.'

'We have one, sir. It's small but clean.'

He nodded. 'My horse needs rubbing down, feeding and stabling.'

'Walter will attend to it.'

3

'See he does it well. The animal is valuable.'

Again she nodded and he drew off his gloves, stretching his cramped legs to the fireplace. Her brown eyes flickered over his elegantly cut but worn doublet of blue velvet. His haughty stare and commanding tone pronounced him gentleman but he lacked gold, that was clear enough.

'Will you take dinner, sir?' She flushed under the scrutiny of those strange, light eyes. She refrained from extolling the quality of the inn's cooking or her own attention to cleanliness. Let him make his own judgement.

He nodded again. 'Ale first, girl, and check attention for my horse.'

She went into the kitchen, deftly avoiding one pair of arms which stole out to trap her. Job Rushton eyed her under heavy brows. He'd been drinking heavily. She'd noted it earlier in the evening. He was now almost too far gone in ale to greet the stranger as he should have done.

'Who is he?'

He'd heard then.

'I don't know. He's strange to these parts, a gentleman.'

He snorted contemptuously. 'Riding unattended? He chooses to lodge here? Gentry he may be, wealthy, never.'

'I did not say that,' she said quietly. ''Tis true he's shabby enough. He's ridden far but he's used to good service.'

4

He shrugged, turning from her to spit into the rushes. 'I leave that to you, but see he pays well.'

She was glad to leave him to his drinking. His huge shambling figure filled her with disgust. What flamboyant good looks the man had possessed when her mother had married him five years ago had long since departed. He ate too much, drank excessively and took little or no exercise. His manners had worsened since her mother's death almost a year ago. Margaret was grudgingly willing to admit he had perhaps loved her gentle mother. Certainly he'd gone to pieces since her passing.

The stranger took a deep pull of the ale. He nodded, satisfied, and she left him to call Walter the ostler to deal with his horse and later to return to the kitchen to prepare his dinner.

It was warm near the fire and Sir Charles Beaumont felt pleasantly drowsy. The dinner was well cooked and served and he lingered for a while afterwards near the hearth before calling the girl to show him to his bed-chamber.

She stooped to light a rush-light from the fire and waited for him to follow. As there seemed no sign of a landlord, he said curtly, 'You are over-young to be in charge of the inn.'

She smiled faintly. 'My step-father, Job Rushton, owns "The Crossed Keys", sir. He's indisposed at present but I assure you I'm well able to take charge for him. I'm almost

5

fourteen.'

He brushed past her to enter the small room at the bend of the stairs, lowering his head under the lintel. She stood in the doorway and lighted the place for him. It was barely furnished but clean scrubbed. He placed a hand on the rough kersey covering of the straw-stuffed mattress and grunted his satisfaction. The sheets smelt fresh and sweet with lavender. This would do very well, much better than expected. He indicated that the girl was to place the rush-light holder on a wooden chest near the bed.

'This is perfectly satisfactory, Mistress—?' He arched one fair eyebrow upwards in a question.

'Mistress Margaret, sir. Margaret Woollat.'

'Very well. I want to be on the road early. I ride to London.'

'I'll see breakfast is ready soon after cock-crow.' Again there was the tired note in her voice though she was as respectful as ever. 'I'll bring water for you, sir. You'll want to wash.'

His lips curved wryly. 'Aye, mistress, I need to wash, as you say.'

When she returned some moments later with water hot from the cauldron over the kitchen fire, he had divested himself of his doublet and stood before her in lawn shirt and hose. She noted the fine quality of the cloth as she offered him a towel. Like the rest of his apparel the shirt was fine but well-worn. She waited

6

attentively while he splashed water over face and hands. He turned smiling, 'That will be all, mistress, thank you.'

His light blue eyes appraised her from top to toe. Her clothing was simple, a kirtle of grey, which appeared to have been made for her some years before. It strained across her high, young breasts, but was scrupulously clean and well darned. A snowy kerchief hid bosom and throat from his view. She was not a beauty but he admired the good lines of her figure and the abundant nut-brown hair, which unlike ladies of fashion at the Burgundian Court, she wore unadorned and tied firmly back with a knot of green ribbon. In the uncertain light her face seemed squarish cut, her chin heavy, almost aggressive, her nose well-shaped but not small. Her mouth was large, almost sulky. He could not tell now while she looked so tired. He judged her complexion to be good and it would show to finer advantage in the fresher light of morning. He gave her a mocking half bow in dismissal.

'Sir Charles Beaumont bids you good night, mistress, and thanks you for your attention.'

She coloured as she realised his intention to strip himself and wash completely. She stammered her apology and left him.

He took advantage of the hot water to cleanse himself thoroughly and rub himself briskly with the rough towel she had provided. It was unlooked for good fortune to find himself accommodation such as this. Relaxed under the pleasant feel of clean sheets, he sighed his relief. The inn was not one used by any who might know him. He could sleep in peace. Tonight there would be little fear of any recognising in him the haughty young squire who had been banished by the King ten years ago. Tomorrow it would not be so simple. He had changed, of course, grown broader; he was less elegantly clad but his hair had retained that golden lightness which had been rare then at the Yorkist court and he was ever twitted about those blue eyes of his, eyes which were idolised by the ladies of his acquaintance. There was no doubt he stood in some danger on this errand. He had cursed himself for a fool many times since the initial decision to come and often later when discomfort and lack of ready gold had added to his irritation during the journey.

The rush-light spluttered and its foul smell annoyed him. He reached over and extinguished it. The girl had been ready to please. He smiled in the darkness. There had been so many inn wenches during those long years and all of them ready to please Charles Beaumont. This one had aroused in him an odd feeling of sympathy. He had had an unusual urge to treat her with respect, a courtesy he bestowed on few; noble ladies or women of more doubtful antecedents. The girl had the air of one who was bred for better things. She had not spoken with the accent of the country maid. He shrugged. God's teeth. Why should the wench intrigue him? There was little beauty that he could detect in that stolid, respectful countenance, not even the cheerful impudence of the typical tavern maid. He doubted if she would offer her favours lightly and Sir Charles Beaumont was not one to sue. At all events, he required no bed-mate tonight. He was weary and he needed all his wits about him on the morrow.

He woke immediately he heard the soft slithering outside his door. He cursed his stupidity in sleeping naked in the bed trusting to the outward respectability of the inn. He reached for his dagger, close to hand under his pillow, and lay still for a moment, waiting. So the rascally innkeeper had lulled him into a false sense of security by the use of his young step-daughter as a front. Beaumont smiled grimly. The man would find a trained mercenary ready and waiting, more than he bargained for. The noise had stopped. No one made an effort to enter. It was pitch black in the room. The moon was not up. If he lighted the rush-light he would warn them he was watchful. He reached for hose and shirt, gripping his dagger between his teeth. He would risk nothing. The door was bolted, that he had made sure of. It was never his custom to sleep in an unbarred room, familiar or not.

The noise recommenced. Someone was

dragging himself farther up the stairs. There was a thumping jar. Whoever he was, was far gone in ale. His progress was unsteady. Apparently he, Beaumont, had been unnecessarily alarmed. He was not the target for the man's stealthy approach. Beaumont completed the tying of his points and donned his doublet. He judged the night young still, but now he was armed and dressed he would remain so. He sat awhile, straining his ears in the darkness. It was no uncommon practice for the customers to be systematically robbed. His turn might yet come, though he doubted the drunken man's intentions. The man was in no fit state to attempt such a task and Beaumont was convinced he had had no accomplices. He was alone when he climbed the stair.

Beaumont's sharp ears caught a soft scratching against a door somewhere above, and the man's ale-thickened tones.

'Meg, let me in.'

So that was it. The ale-sot required a bed-mate. Beaumont lay full out again on the bed. No concern of his. He would sleep again. He sorely needed it. Then he frowned. From whom was the man demanding favours, the girl, the innkeeper's step-daughter? 'May he rot in hell,' Beaumont muttered, 'the drunken swine. She's not for him.'

Obviously the anxious swain had not been admitted for he scratched again and his whines could be heard even from this distance.

'Meg, it's me, Job. Undo the door, girl. I've a matter of some importance to discuss with you.'

The girl's answer was inaudible but apparently it was in the negative for the innkeeper, as Beaumont now judged him to be, swore roundly and thundered on the door.

Beaumont sat up again and sighed. He would get little rest tonight, it was plain. Should he bellow to the drunken oaf and order him to let peaceful customers rest?

By now the man was raining heavy blows on the girl's door. He must have placed his shoulder against it for there was a crash and a shrill cry. Beaumont waited for no more. He rarely interfered in the amorous practices of others but it was clear to him that the girl was distressed and unused to coping with circumstances such as this. He'd wring the brute's neck and throw him down-stairs to cool off a while. Perhaps then he'd get some sleep. He went barefoot to his own door, drew back the bolts quietly and ran lightly up the upper stairway. From the room he could hear the girl's pleading, the man's heavy breathing and the scuffles of two struggling creatures. Even now the girl kept her voice low for fear of waking the customer who slept below them.

The man had forced the girl backwards over the bed. He was muttering sickening protestations of love. She had kindled the rush-light and by its glimmer Beaumont saw

11

her fighting desperately. Her shift was torn. The man's back was to him.

'Let the wench go.' Beaumont's tone was contemptuous.

The man's grip on the girl loosened. He turned heavily, as if surprised. Ale had slowed his wits. The girl gave a sob, half of distress and embarrassment, half of heart-felt gratitude.

'Eh?' The man's voice was bewildered. 'What did you say?'

'Let her go. You're not wanted, my friend.'

'What in the name of all the devils in hell has it to do with you?' The man's bluster became more confident. 'This is my house, the girl's mine. Get about your own business. Leave me to mine.'

A more cautious man might have heeded the glitter in Beaumont's blue eyes. He came nearer. He did not raise his voice.

'I choose to make this my business. Get out and leave the girl, I say. Are there no wenches in the village that will take you?'

The man's features flooded red with fury at the calculated insult. Bull-like he lunged at the intruder. Beaumont caught him easily in a trained wrestler's grip, strained one arm behind his back and tightened. The man gave an animal yelp of pain. Contemptuously Beaumont released him and Job Rushton collapsed like a sack of flour at his feet and doubled over moaning feebly.

Beaumont went to the bed-side and seized a

12

blanket. 'Cover yourself and come with me, mistress,' he said quietly. 'He'll not hurt you this night. Later he'll sober up, never fear.'

The light caught her terrified face, mouth open as if in a silent cry, hair dishevelled and tumbling over her bare shoulders in a riot of soft brown waves. She reached to take the blanket from him, then suddenly her dark eyes dilated. Warned, he swung round to find the innkeeper had risen and was advancing, a heavy iron-studded stool raised above his head. One blow from that would have cracked Beaumont's skull. Beaumont aimed and threw. Not once had he put down his weapon. The innkeeper gave a second gurgling cry as the dagger buried itself in his breast. He sank this time like a stone.

Beaumont turned once more to the girl. 'Dress,' he said harshly. 'Leave him to me.'

The man was breathing but losing blood heavily. A couple of inches to the right and he would never have risen again, but as it was he would give no more trouble tonight, though later he'd ruffle it again among the womenfolk. Beaumont seized a sheet, tore it into strips, made one into a pad, withdrew his dagger blade and bound the pad into place to control the bleeding. The man was still unconscious but, to be sure of no more interference, Beaumont seized the remaining sheet, ripped it expertly into two strong ropes and tied the man's wrists and ankles.

'Have you killed him?' He looked up into the pale blur of the girl's face. Her voice was controlled but he saw she was near to breaking point. She'd obeyed him and was now fully dressed.

He shook his head. 'No. It's a relief, since I have no desire to have the village constable at my heels. This wound will keep him bedded for a while, that's all.'

She murmured a soft prayer. Was it in gratitude? He couldn't tell. She looked round the little room in a gesture of panic. She was clutching one wrist as if it pained her. He stood up and came to her, taking the injured wrist in his long, brown fingers and feeling gently for broken bones. She winced at the pressure but made no outcry.

'It's naught but a sprain, mistress, no bones broken.'

'Thank you.' Her eyes were bright with unshed tears. Gently but firmly she withdrew her hand from his grasp. 'It seems little to say. He ... he ... has been drinking all day and ...' Her voice broke. 'I ... I think all will be well tomorrow when he recovers.'

'I think not, mistress.' She looked up into his stern arrogant face and made a little helpless shrug.

'I ... can do nothing. I ...'

'If you don't want his attentions and it's plain you don't, you must leave here.'

Her eyes widened again and hope flared in

14

them like a beacon.

He smiled in answer to her unspoken question. 'I'll escort you part of the way at least.'

She made no useless protestations or exclamations of gratitude.

'I'll pack some necessities,' she said simply. 'I've little enough. I'll take nothing of his.'

He warmed to her determination. 'Who else sleeps in the inn? It seems silent now as the grave.'

'No one. Walter the ostler sleeps in the stable, though like as not he'll still be wenching in the village. You are our only guest.'

He nodded. 'I'll collect my baggage and saddle my horse.' He followed her glance down to her step-father's supine body. 'He'll not bleed to death. He'll do till the morning. We must be well away by then. Be ready very soon.'

'I'll not delay you.' He gripped her uninjured hand to show his confidence and left her.

There seemed no sign of the ostler in the stable. Phoebus stood docilely enough while he saddled up. He'd already packed and was not booted and spurred for the journey. He led the horse out into the courtyard and prepared to call the girl.

Almost in answer to his thought she came quietly to his side, cloaked, her brown hair covered with a drab hood. He took her bundle from her and fastened it with his own saddle-

15

bag, then mounted and reached down his hand.

She turned and looked once at the inn then came up behind him. He felt her young body, clean and fresh close against his own as he fastened her arms round his waist. Without another word he spurred his mount out of the inn-yard and on to the London road.

CHAPTER TWO

The sound of violent splashing further upstream woke Beaumont to grey skies above and a cold snap in the air. The fire he had made last night had evidently been remade for it was blazing well. The girl was nowhere in sight. He concluded it was her he could hear washing in the stream. She had folded her cloak neatly over the bundle which had served her for a pillow during the night. He struggled up and looked for more twigs for the fire, rubbing his hands and stamping his feet to restore the circulation.

'God's teeth, why had he burdened himself with the girl?' Hers was a fate common to inn wenches. He had merely put it off for some time, meanwhile what was he to do with her? Phoebus could carry the two of them without difficulty but in London he had problems enough to face. He *could* have spent last night comfortably warm in the inn instead of sleeping under the bushes in this small copse and it was likely enough they would be pursued, though he had ridden some miles from 'The Crossed Keys' and it had been well after midnight before he had halted Phoebus to rest here under cover of the trees and some way clear of the main highway. He had no wish to draw attention to himself before he reached his destination.

He turned as a twig snapped behind him and she came to the fire. He was ashamed of his irritation. Last night she'd been so sensible in spite of her fear, that he'd forgotten how young she was. Now, her face scrubbed clean and shining from the icy water, her brown hair plaited and tied back with the knot of green ribbon, she looked a mere child. She smiled shyly at him, and he cursed his frowning countenance as she said, 'I have caused you discomfort, sir. Had you not come to my help, you would not have had to sleep out cold and stiff. The wind is still icy though it's well into March.'

'Come and warm yourself for a moment while I go and wash. We must find some inconspicuous tavern for breakfast. I'm anxious for us not to be recognised for some hours at least. We must get a fair start.'

'I brought food from the inn while you saddled up.'

He turned and grinned at her. 'Sensible girl,

lay it out. I could eat my horse which would be unwise.'

It was a frugal but satisfying meal of bread, cold meat and cheese. An ale flagon had been impossible to carry. It had always been his custom to carry a metal drinking cup and he fetched water from the stream. It was enough.

He threw more sticks on the fire as she huddled close, toasting her toes against its warmth. 'Your step-father called you Meg.'

She nodded. 'To the village folk I'm Meg. My father always called me Margaret and so I was to all on London Bridge.'

'Ah, you were born in the city. I thought so. I judge by your accent.'

'You live in London?' She turned to him eagerly.

'I *did*, some time ago.'

'Oh.' It was apparent she was curious and he said, 'I have been in Burgundy for almost nine years. I have business in London.'

Her eyes appealed but she hesitated before speaking aloud.

His mouth twisted wryly. 'I will take you as far as the outskirts at least. Later it might not be wise for you to be seen with me.' As her eyes opened wide with wonder he continued, 'I was banished. Were I recognised and arrested, I *could* go to the block.'

She busied herself in tidying away the remains of their meal. He frowned. Her ability to keep a close mouth was disconcerting and

18

unchildlike. 'I fought a duel to the death. It was forbidden by the rules of the tournament. My rival had won the hand of the lady I desired to marry.'

'You killed him?' This time she betrayed more human curiosity.

He shook his head. 'He near damn well killed me.'

'You loved his lady, truly?'

Again that cynical twist of the lips. 'Hardly. She was very young, scarce older than you are now, but she was an heiress. However, I lost her and was forbidden the realm. I have lived since as a hired mercenary. I see your eyes judged the cut of my cloth last night.'

She coloured. 'My father, Tom Woollat, was a cloth merchant. I came to know and evaluate the worth of cloths.'

'Your mother remarried recently? That brute?'

'He was not always so. She was lonely. He lived then in London. He was handsome in a cheap, flamboyant way. He made much of her, flattered her, gave her gifts, of little value true, but she missed my father. She married him five years ago and he bought "The Crossed Keys" and we came here. I think mother preferred to live far from her old friends, you understand?'

'Yes. You are her only child?'

'Yes. I had a brother. He died of plague.'

'And Job Rushton has treated you ill?'

'Only recently. Mother died about a year

ago. He's gone downhill since, sampled his own wares too frequently.'

'What will you do now? Have you friends in London? It's no place for a girl as young as you without protectors.'

She lowered her head. 'You think I'm likely to end in the stews on Bankside? I'll not do that. No, I've no one I would ask for help. Mother's friends warned her against Job. My pride won't let me go to them. I can get work in some inn. I'm experienced.' She looked up at his silence and jutted her chin obstinately at his amused smile.

'I think you are not—experienced.' He rose abruptly. 'Well we must see what we can do for you, Mistress Woollat. I'll cover the fire then we'll make a start. We should reach London before nightfall.'

She was very silent during the journey. They had one meal at an inn some three miles from the city. She looked uncomfortable when he ordered for both of them. He laughed at her discomfiture, 'Come, mistress, are you afraid I cannot pay my reckoning? Mercenaries are not so ill-paid as that.'

'I have some money and some trinkets my father gave me.'

'And you must keep them. You may well need them.'

She persisted no longer. It pleased him to see the colour come back to her face as she ate and drank. Never before had the company of a

20

maid given him so rare a pleasure. She trusted him utterly yet she made no attempt at useless chatter but sat quietly waiting until he was ready to resume their journey.

Now as they entered the city he felt her arms tighten apprehensively round his waist. It was already dark and his horse stumbled. The wind had come up though the afternoon had been sunny. It would be a cold night. The streets were almost deserted. He peered about him in the gloom for familiar landmarks. The city seemed unchanged. In the Chepe he drew up by the lighted courtyard of 'The Golden Cockerel'. Something stirred in his memory as he noted the swinging sign, but he shook his head. He could not recollect visiting the place. There should be no one here who knew him from the old days.

Before she dismounted, he heard Margaret Woollat whisper, 'You are sure it is safe for you, sir?'

'As safe as any place here, my beauty. Down you go.'

A pleasant-faced wench came to greet him in the tap-room. She looked curiously at his companion when he asked for two rooms.

'If only one is available I'll sleep in a common room,' he said quickly. 'My cousin is very tired. Could you serve dinner early and allow her to go to bed?'

'Certainly, sir. We have what you require. Come close to the fire. The night is chill.'

21

He drew Margaret to the table near the fire and chafed her cold hands. Her child's eyes roamed the prosperous inn parlour. 'The Golden Cockerel' was larger than 'The Crossed Keys' and boasted several servants. A jovial innkeeper came to their side as one of the maids laid dinner before them.

'The beds will be well aired, sir, never fear, and spotlessly clean.'

Beaumont speared portions of fowl on to Margaret's trencher. 'I can judge that from the service here.'

'You were recommended to me, sir, Jake Garnet of "The Golden Cockerel"?'

Beaumont again looked up as the name stirred a chord in his memory, but the man's deep bass tones and his round shining countenance were completely unfamiliar. He smiled. 'My comrades have mentioned the place.'

'Good, good. You are from the North?'

Beaumont did not look at him again. 'Not recently,' he said quietly. 'We may stay some days. I have business here.'

'May I hope it will be profitable.' The man moved off and Beaumont signed his young companion to eat. She did so though with less heartiness than formerly. He laughed aloud at her woebegone expression.

'Come, Margaret, what fears have you? This is a respectable inn.'

'You will not endanger yourself unduly?'

'I certainly will not. I value my skin.'

'Do you?' she hesitated then plunged on, 'do you hope to kill your opponent at last?'

He checked, gulped his wine, choked, then set down his tankard.

'My good girl of course not. I should be somewhat late. They've been wed these eight years.'

Her grave expression did not lighten and he leaned back in his chair. 'No child, I came to see someone.'

'Someone you love?'

'Not exactly. Someone I should *like* to love.'

She turned from him then, unwilling to question him further.

He sat in the pleasant warmth from the fire, dreaming into his mulled wine, his thoughts ranging back over the years. It was a pity that he must leave London again so soon. Tomorrow his friend should still be on duty. He was in good time. His errand over, he must make all speed for Dover again. He looked across at the girl. She seemed half asleep, her hand gently curving round the handle of her tankard. Somehow he must ensure her decent employment. There were men he knew who would take her into kitchen service but he had no wish to involve any of them with knowledge of his whereabouts at this time. This inn seemed respectable. He could have approached the innkeeper. He had of course mentioned the girl as his cousin but it was

23

unlikely that tale had been believed.

He leaned over and touched her lightly on the arm. She jumped, her hand flying to her mouth to stifle a cry of alarm. At sight of him smiling genially at her across the table, she relaxed.

'It is late, mistress. I'll call the maid to see you to your chamber.'

A dull flush suffused her face and throat. 'You stay awhile, sir?'

'Just a while longer to drowse over more wine.'

'I ... you ...' she floundered in acute misery, 'you said just now I lack experience, sir. I know that is true, but ... but I will try to please you if ...'

'Mistress Margaret, you honour me greatly and I thank you.' His words were gravely courteous. 'But I cannot accept your generous offer. You are very tired. I bespoke a private chamber for you.'

'You don't want me?' The words were whispered in an agony of self-shame.

He avoided her dark eyes and controlled with difficulty the desire to laugh. Not for the world would he hurt her thus. 'Would you have me do what I punished another for attempting?'

She glanced suspiciously at his raised fair eyebrows. 'No.'

'You are very young, my dear. I have enjoyed your company. In that I have been

24

more than repaid. Now go, you need sleep.'

For a moment he thought she would make some retort. Her lovely eyes flashed at him as if to repudiate her childish status, then she rose and swept him a courtly curtsey.

'Good night, sir. I thank you for your protection. You need have no further fears for me. I'll find work in the morning and I can pay my reckoning.'

'So anxious to be rid of me, mistress,' he chided her mockingly.

Again she flushed, made to speak, thought better of it, and as he signalled a maid who approached his table, she followed the girl from the tap-room.

He sat on for a while, determined to allow her time to retire before he left for his own chamber. At last he summoned the landlord who was passing after bidding good night to a wealthy merchant at the door of the inn.

'Sir?' the man waited by the table politely.

'I shall leave the inn early, possibly before my companion awakes. Do not allow her to pay any part of our reckoning. That I will discharge in full and—' he paused and looked at the other meaningly, 'I would be grateful if you could find some means to delay her departure until I return.'

'I understand, sir.'

Beaumont stroked the side of his nose thoughtfully. 'The lady is anxious to get decent employment. She has worked in an inn and is capable. She also has good knowledge of cloths and weaves.'

'Indeed, sir. I'll give the matter some thought. My daughter may know someone who would take her in. You intend to leave London?'

'Within two or three days.'

'Were you not squire to the Duke of Clarence, sir?'

Beaumont's blue eyes flashed oddly. He peered closely at the man's round, open countenance. 'You recognise me?'

'No, sir. I think we never met. I knew well Sir Piers Langham. His lady, Mistress Alicia Standish, gave me the honour of her patronage. I was an archer in her father's company at Wakefield.'

'Of course.' Beaumont gave a short laugh, 'I remember now. Langham often came to this inn when we were squires together at Baynards Castle. It seems long ago.'

'To you, sir, perhaps.'

Beaumont traced a finger in a pool of spilt wine on the scrubbed table-top. 'You have word of Lady Alicia?'

'Aye, sir. She's well and the mother of two fine children, a lad almost six years old now named Richard for his Grace of Gloucester, and little Anne was born two years ago. They spend most of their time at Middleham where Sir Piers serves in his Grace's household or on Sir Piers's estate in Kent.'

26

'And she is happy?'

'She was radiant when last I saw her.'

'I'm glad all is well with them.' He pursed his lips. 'You know then, I have no right to be here.'

The smile left the innkeeper's face. He looked gravely at his guest. 'Mean you ill to the King's cause, sir?'

'Would you believe me if I said "no"?'

'Aye, sir, that I would. Sir Piers speaks well of you. What was between you is over long ago. If you have need to come to London, I'll not blab of your presence here. You can be sure of that.'

Beaumont stood up, stretching his tall frame to his full height. 'I thank you, Jake Garnet. I'd be glad of your good offices for the lady and when next you see Sir Piers and Lady Langham give them my best regards and congratulate them on their fine children.'

'That I will, Sir Charles.'

'And now, man, I'll to bed. Clean sheets will be a luxury. My chamber last night was too noisy and disturbed and later too cold.'

The man's respectful expression betrayed no idle curiosity.

Beaumont leaned over and squeezed his arm, then strode off to seek his own chamber.

CHAPTER THREE

'It's as well you came today.' Sir John Gaveston led the way up the stone stairway, pausing for Beaumont to catch up with him. 'At any time the children are to be moved.'

Beaumont stopped and stared out over the Tower gardens through an arrow slit. Two ravens swooped down on to the lawn. He shuddered in spite of himself. The black-coated birds seemed harbingers of evil. 'They are leaving the Tower?'

'It's not sure yet. Dorset has charge of them. Why he should wish to burden himself I cannot imagine.'

Beaumont's lips tightened. 'That is just as well, my friend. I'm grateful that you arrange this for me. You take grave risks.'

The other man reached over and took his old friend's arm in a grasp of affection. 'Clarence was good to both of us in the old days. I deserved many a beating I did not get. I don't forget.'

'Yet he could be cruel enough.'

'Aye.' Gaveston sighed. 'It's a hard world and not meant for sensitive men. Were I one, I'd shave my head and enter the nearest monastery. There was little real malice in him. The man was a fool.' He stopped suddenly at Beaumont's sharp intake of breath. 'You'll not deny it, Charles. Edward's easy going but not when his crown's threatened.'

'It went as far as that?'

'Clarence challenged him to single combat before what was virtually an assembly of Parliament.'

'Unwise.' Beaumont smiled bleakly. 'I was banished for challenging a favourite. Even the Duke of Clarence should have thought twice before issuing such an invitation to the King's Grace.'

'They bellowed and screamed at each other for over an hour. It was obvious in the end that even Gloucester would be unable to save him.'

'He tried then? I had not heard that.'

'He travelled hard from Middleham. He might well have succeeded. The King held his hand before fixing the date of execution even after judgement went against him, then, as you know, the Duke was found dead.'

'Of drinking too much of his favourite malmsey.'

Gaveston cast him a side-long glance. 'His death may have been in the cup. Who knows? I judged it not prudent to enquire further. Even Gloucester saw the wisdom in that.'

'It has taken me these many months to leave Burgundy. Dangerous as it is, I had to reassure myself about the children.'

'You'll have this time alone with them. I've dismissed their servants. You won't be disturbed. I'll be within call. The little lass will

29

be delighted to see you. She welcomes any new experience.'

'And the young Earl?'

The other shrugged. 'He's still little more than a baby. They both favour the Plantagenets in colouring.'

Beaumont frowned as his friend unbarred the heavy door at the head of the stairs and gestured him to enter. It seemed a high, desolate prison for two small children. He was relieved to discover that the room was pleasant enough, a brazier gave warmth and the spring sunlight flooded in through an enlarged arrow slit which had been paned with glass. Some efforts had been made to ensure comfort for the King's young guests.

A stern-faced woman rose from her spinning near the window and a child, who had been standing by her side, watching, turned and ran towards Sir John. He caught her up and turned to face Beaumont.

'You have a visitor, Lady Margaret. You must curtsey becomingly. Are you not a princess?' She snuggled against his shoulder, then held out one dainty little hand towards Beaumont.

'May I present Sir Charles Beaumont, sir, a former squire of your father.' Gaveston placed The Lady Margaret down gently and crossed to the table where a small boy sat on a stool which had been raised by cushions so that he might reach. He was peering down at a piece of parchment, protected by horn on which had been written in huge letters, his name, 'Edward'. He made no effort to jump down from the stool, and only turned his head when Sir John went to his side and touched his shoulder gently.

Beaumont angrily forced back a sudden rush of tears. The little girl had taken his hand and was smiling at him, her curiosity at the sight of a new face replacing former shyness. She was already a little beauty with the red-gold hair and pink and white complexion of both Nevilles and Plantagenets. He could picture in her little of the fragility of her mother, The Lady Isobel, elder of the Kingmaker's daughters. The boy stared at him vacantly out of bright blue eyes. Beaumont was appalled at the lack of interest. He drew in his lips as if the effort of transferring his attention from his letters required some physical reaction, then he looked up again at Sir John for guidance.

Gaveston dismissed the nurse. 'Come back in an hour, Gertrude. I'll not leave the children without summoning you.'

She curtseyed, her black, shrewd eyes appraising the visitor, then left, drawing the door to behind her.

The Lady Margaret did not give her a parting glance. There seemed little affection between them. Beaumont smiled down at her and undid the linen bundle he had brought with him. She snatched at his hand and he

31

laughed aloud at her normal, childish lack of good manners. The crudely carved, painted wooden doll brought a cry of delight. She sat down where she was on the rushes to hold it close and croon to it, its donor immediately forgotten. Gaveston did not reprove her. He looked gravely across at Beaumont, from his position by the Earl, and frowning, shook his head.

Sir Charles remained where he was and held out his gift. The boy's eyes travelled slowly down the length of the specially made bow with its brightly painted quiver. As the child made no move to jump down from his stool and take the gift, Beaumont came nearer. The boy showed no instinctive fear of him. Those strange almost unseeing eyes continued to regard him, unfocused like those of a baby, then he turned back to the parchment page and carefully began to trace one finger round the first of the letters. Sir Charles placed his gift on the table within the boy's view.

Gaveston cleared his throat. 'The Lord Edward will play with the bow perhaps tomorrow if the weather is fine. We thank you, Sir Charles, do we not Lady Margaret?'

The older child sprang up at once and ran to Beaumont. She said with old-world preciseness, 'I do indeed thank you, sir, for my brother and myself. It is good of you to call and see us.'

He knelt and kissed the tips of her dimpled

fingers and she blushed up at him rosily. She was a delightful child, utterly unspoilt and apparently completely trusting.

Gaveston followed his gaze to the boy's bent head. Beaumont realised it would be useless to formally pay his respects. His task was done. He had seen Clarence's children. He would not embarrass John Gaveston by his presence here any longer.

'Thank you, Sir John. I will take my leave if her Grace will excuse me.'

She bowed her golden head regally, but it was plain she were now anxious to return to her new toy and would not miss the company of either of them.

Gaveston went to the door. 'I'll summon their nurse.' Before he could reach it, the door was opened and a man stepped into the room. Gaveston was about to reprove his interruption, then stopped and bowed low.

'Good morning, Sir John.' The newcomer stripped off his gloves, then stared into the eyes of Sir Charles Beaumont. A puzzled flicker moved those cool, grey eyes, then suddenly he was almost bowled over by the rapturous greeting of the little Lady Margaret.

'My Lord Uncle, they did not tell me you were to come to see us. Oh, it's good to see you.'

He stooped to lift her to his shoulder, rumpling her tumbled curls. She was still clutching the doll and she held it up now for his

33

inspection.

'*He* brought it.' She stabbed a decisive finger at Beaumont who stood guiltily irresolute, 'and a bow for Edward and he has not *looked* at it or given his thanks. Is it not wrong of Edward?'

Her second visitor held her still closer. 'We'll examine it more closely, sweet coz, in one moment and Edward is busy, it seems, at his lessons, but first let us take our leave of this gentleman.'

Beaumont found the presence of mind to bow. He had been too taken aback at the appearance of the Royal Duke that he had not the wit to speak or move.

'Your pardon, My Lord of Gloucester,' he said quietly, 'with your leave.'

Gloucester nodded and swept over to the table to speak with his nephew. If he were angered to find Beaumont there, he made no sign.

'I'll see you before I leave, Gaveston,' he said as that officer drew Beaumont to the door of the chamber and down the stone stair.

'Are the children forbidden visitors?' Grim-faced Beaumont questioned him outside the tower.

Gaveston shook his head. 'No official order has been made. God's death, what a pass that Gloucester should appear. I thought him in the North.'

'The Lady Margaret seems fond of him.'

'Aye, she is.'

'And the Earl?'

Gaveston turned his head away to avoid Beaumont's eyes. 'You saw how it is with him. But what of you? Did Gloucester know you, do you think?'

'It would be strange if he did not. We are old enemies.'

'Enemies?' The other's tone was sharp.

'I did him once the greatest injury one man may do another—except perhaps to take his life. I must leave, my friend. God guard you. I fear you may be called to account for this day's work.'

'That cannot be helped. I love the children as you do. You saw for yourself that they are well cared for and healthy.'

'For how long under my lord The Marquess of Dorset?'

Gaveston's dark eyes sought his own uneasily. 'I cannot think the King's stepson would harm the children, they are his cousins by marriage.'

'Aye, so they are.'

Beaumont clapped a hand on his friend's shoulder. They looked at each other for a moment without speaking, then abruptly Gaveston walked with him towards the guard at the main entrance gate.

Beaumont had walked the short distance to the Tower. He quickened his steps in the direction of the inn, pausing once only in a cloth-merchant's shop to buy Margaret a new kerchief of linen. It was embroidered and would please her, he felt sure, for he judged she had received few presents during recent years. He was anxious to see her safely bestowed before he left London. Now it was more urgent than ever that he left early tomorrow or even tonight and slept well out of the city. He cursed his bad luck in an encounter with Gloucester, he of all men.

Gloucester had been present at that fatal tournament, when he like a crass fool had challenged Sir Piers Langham to combat to death. They had all been there, Edward, the King, Clarence his own master, flushed with drinking, his Lady Isobel, Gloucester and his newly betrothed Anne Neville, Warwick's younger daughter, she who had disappeared so mysteriously from Clarence's household and been discovered working as a cook-maid in the Chepe. Now she was Gloucester's Duchess with a son of her own, queening it at her father's castle of Middleham which together with his possessions at Sherrifs Hutton had been given to her as part of her shared inheritance with her sister, Isobel, Duchess of Clarence. How furious Clarence had been that day; his own wishes frustrated, part of the Warwick fortune given into Richard's keeping in spite of all his efforts to retain it.

How well Beaumont recalled the pageantry and splendour of that day. The King had held

36

the jousts at Smithfield in honour of his victory at Tewkesbury. He, Beaumont, like Clarence, his master, nursed a sick hatred. Had not Alicia Standish been given to that Stable Knight, Sir Piers Langham, and she formerly promised to him by Warwick her guardian. All that had come to naught when Warwick was slain at Barnet. God knew he needed her inheritance.

So they fought; Langham for all his yeoman stock had acted like a gentleman. He'd spared his life and strangely, there at the last they'd vowed friendship. Once or twice he'd heard from his opponent but he himself had been hard to trace, moving lodgings as he had constantly during his service with Charles of Burgundy.

In Clarence's service he'd blackened Gloucester's name to Anne, convinced her that the Duke had slain Edward of Wales after Tewkesbury, though for all he knew the prince had been slain in the retreat. And she believed him and trusted to Clarence. Beaumont did not doubt that he might have sent that frail girl to her death, yet Gloucester had found her and wed her. Truth to say he had no cause to love Charles Beaumont and no reason to forget him. Since the King had forbidden him the realm, if he were taken, it would go ill with him. Yet he must see Margaret Woollat settled first. Assured of that, he would leave England's shores without regret. What he had seen today in that little tower room had saddened him beyond thought. His hopes were gone. Clarence's son would never fulfil those high hopes he, Beaumont, had had for him.

He was nearing 'The Golden Cockerel' now. The Tower visit had taken longer than he anticipated. It would be unlikely that Garnet, the innkeeper, would have been able to prevent Margaret from leaving the inn. He hoped the man would have had the sense to at least discover where she had gone. This morning over breakfast, he'd mentioned the possibility of service for her with a cloth merchant of his acquaintance.

The jingle of harness made him suddenly alert. The people who had pressed him close to the narrow streets had been merchants, apprentices, even one or two noblemen. He had seen few soldiers and those he might have met would have been intent on pleasure in the taverns and brothels, and would hardly be armed and spurred. He stopped for a moment at a goldsmith's open-fronted shop to peer inside, then turned his head to the street behind. Three men, armed, one obviously an officer, intent on business were following close. He swore aloud then moved onwards forcing his brain to work at lightning speed. Gloucester had undoubtedly given the order for his arrest the moment he left the Tower. He had delayed to speak to John Gaveston and yet again when he bought the embroidered kerchief. It had given time for the guard to catch up with him and follow. Whatever he did, he must not go near 'The Golden Cockerel'. Margaret Woollat could not be connected with him. Even suspicion of complicity might endanger her. If he could, he would throw off his pursuers, if not he must trust to his experience in hand-to-hand combat. He wore no sword today but he carried his dagger strapped in his sleeve, in its usual position. No mercenary trusted even his companions. He was outnumbered three to one but he had coped with such odds before and come out of it victorious, but there was no chance here in this street. If fight he must, then he'd choose his own territory, an alley where he could lie in wait behind a corner or low gable and ambush his attackers. Only an element of surprise would aid him now.

It was crowded in the street. He whispered up a prayer of gratitude. He was not conspicuously dressed. It was not difficult to lose himself among the townsfolk who thronged round the shops. Many had over-imbibed in the ins, since it was now past dinner time. They cannoned their way along impervious to the curses and angry glances cast at them. Beaumont twisted and snaked his way through the buyers, good humouredly elbowing past one unsteady one, who attempted to halt him to whisper bawdy phrases in his ear.

Ahead was an alley, well known in the old

days. Standing back from the street was a house well used by some of the wealthy young noblemen. They were forbidden to cross to the stews under threats of beating by their respective masters, who took responsibility for the well-being of their squires, but this served its purpose discreetly. He had visited it more than once but it would be close-shuttered at this time, its business being accomplished at night. He slipped into the shadow of an overhanging gable and drew his dagger from its sheath.

For some moments he thought he might have lost his opponents for there was no betraying jingle of harness, then he heard the sound again and the officer's voice.

'He went this way, I'm sure, Will, you go on and signal if you see him ahead. We'll try the alley.'

Beaumont's curious eyes flickered. If one man was deployed to search, the odds against him were lessened. He could deal with a third, later.

The officer's boots rang on the cobbles. His footsteps sounded less sure now as he moved into the alley and looked round. He had come into the shade and blinked in an effort to adapt his eyes to the gloomier area. There was a flash of steel. He gave a cry and stumbled against the shop wall, Beaumont's dagger in his back. The other man came on at a rush, his feet slithering on the greasy cobbles. Beaumont was now without a weapon. He threw himself at the other man and grabbed for his throat. His pursuer was burly, but not slow on his feet, and no novice at the game. He grunted his rage, evaded Beaumont's grasp and kicked upwards viciously. Beaumont dodged and the other stumbled but as he recovered, he drew his sword and, turning, stood waiting, his breath coming in gasps. He had all the advantage. He needed only to advance. Beaumont watched the man's blade warily. In the whole encounter no one had said a word. The captain had not even called on him to surrender himself to rightful arrest. Beaumont, even at this moment, allowed himself an inward grin. He'd given the man no time to do so, but rendered him *hors de combat*, before they began. His only chance lay now in the other overreaching himself. He retreated gradually, watching for an opportunity to catch the man's attention, take him unawares and make the dangerous attempt to disarm him. The other was taking no chances. He was a tough middle-aged soldier with years of experience. He was not to be easily thrown off-balance by any tricks. Desperation was clouding Beaumont's brain. He had no wish for the man to kill him. If needs must, he would surrender. There was still a chance he might be pardoned. Only if he could come out of this unscathed would he risk jumping his opponent.

The other advanced methodically, his eyes

41

watchful, Beaumont continued to watch his blade, then without warning he felt a grip of steel on his right ankle. Too late he remembered his fallen adversary. He remembered giving a cry of mingled surprise and fear and fell heavily. Before he could struggle to his knees he felt an agonising blow on his skull, red lights flashing across his vision, then blackness.

CHAPTER FOUR

Beaumont came painfully to consciousness. It was pitch black around him. He put up a hand to the back of his head and drew it away sticky with blood. He had been out for some time for it was undoubtedly night unless he had been confined in some cell without arrow slit or underground. That was unlikely. Surely his crime had not been so heinous. He stood up, though the action was unwise for he felt immediately sick and faint. Now his eyes were accustoming themselves to darkness he could see a faint greyness to his right. That was the window, sure enough, and there were rushes underfoot and on the bench where they'd thrown him. He was not chained to the wall. Either his captors' orders had not included such treatment or he'd been considered too sick for the present to make any attempt at escape. Not that any were possible.

He stood up again to explore with outstretched finger-tips. His cell was not small. He blundered up against a heavy wooden table and there was a stool. Obviously he was in the Tower, but not yet treated as a common prisoner. He could just glimpse an earthen pitcher on the table. He lifted it and drank the welcome cold water gratefully. There was no sound from outside. It would be useless to thunder on the door, call the jailor and demand to know where he was and on what charge. The man would tell him nothing at this hour and would be unnecessarily angered. Beaumont had learned to keep on the better side of jailors. He winced again as excruciating pains shot through his head. He would lie down again and try to sleep. Nothing could be discovered until the morning and in the meantime he could recover his strength.

For a while sleep eluded him though the pains were less severe now he was resting again. What of Margaret Woollat? Would she think he had deserted her? Strange how he detested the thought. The girl was a burden to him, yet he would have her continue to think well of him. Jake Garnet would not throw her out of the inn without waiting for news. He cursed his stupidity in not paying the man something in advance, yet his horse was still stabled at 'The Golden Cockerel' and his belongings still in his chamber. This signified his intention to return and pay their reckoning. He trusted the man's kindly intention.

So he had not killed the officer? Perhaps that was as well. The charge against him would have been murder of the King's guard. He frowned. The men had not worn Gloucester's livery. He was sure of that. When he'd faced that second guard he'd seen the King's personal cognizance of suns and roses. So Gloucester had been escorted by a company of the King's men and not his own. Likely enough, since he probably came straight from the palace at Westminster. Beaumont sighed and stretched himself on the rushes. There was little chance of appealing to the King's mercy. Gloucester had no reason to forgive him aught. His life was forfeit, since he was forbidden the realm on pain of death.

Experience had taught him never to despair. Despite the uneasy feeling in the pit of his stomach, he forced himself to relax his fear-tightened muscles and sleep at last.

He was shaken roughly awake and found spring sunlight flooding the room. He closed his eyes hastily again for a second as the pain in his head returned. It was not so intense and he sat up experimentally. His jailor was a burly fellow but genial enough. His mouth broadened in a grin as Beaumont felt his head wound carefully.

'Some ale, sir. It's poor stuff but if I'm any judge your mouth'll be like a sand pit. There's bread and cheese. Make a quick meal. You're summoned to the Lieutenant's lodging.'

Beaumont took a deep pull of the ale but waved away the platter of food.

'Water, man, to refresh me, if you will.'

'Aye, sir.'

Beaumont plunged his face in the basin of icy water, gasped, spluttered and felt nearly himself again. He smoothed his hair as best he could and nodded to the jailor to take him to his interrogator.

He was not surprised to find Richard of Gloucester seated at the lieutenant of the Tower's table, his back to the fire. It was still chill in the stone-built room. Winter was giving up his hold but slowly this year of 1479.

'Good morning, Sir Charles. I see Job Wyatt was not the only one who came badly from your encounter yesterday. You will feel better if you sit, I think, there on the stool before me. However, he is mending, I trust you are also doing so.'

Beaumont sat gratefully. He gave a thin smile. 'I didn't kill him then?'

'No, you omitted to finish him which is fortunate since his widow might howl for your blood. In that case the King would have no alternative but to condemn you to the block.'

Beaumont gazed fearlessly back at the Duke. 'Is not that his intention, since you ordered my arrest, your Grace?'

'I?' Gloucester inclined one eyebrow in

45

surprise. 'You wrong me, Beaumont. I had no hand in your arrest. It seems your former acquaintance Sir Thomas Vaughan informed the Lord Chamberlain of your presence in London, reminded him of your banishment and Lord Hastings could do naught but order your imprisonment, pending the King's pleasure.'

'Vaughan?' Beaumont's mouth twisted wryly. 'We were old rivals. But when did he see me?'

Gloucester shrugged. 'I have no idea. Since the guard had orders to proceed to "The Golden Cockerel" it seems you must have been recognised at your lodging.' He poured wine into a goblet and held it towards the prisoner. 'This is better stuff than your jailor provided. It will warm you.'

Beaumont took the wine-cup with a faint bow. The Duke was right. The wine was good. He felt it course through his body giving warmth and almost immediate strength.

He considered the man before him thoughtfully. Gloucester was elegantly dressed in a doublet of blue velvet and hat of the same colour. He wore a gold collar of linked enamelled York roses from which his personal device of the white boar descended. His hair had darkened and was cut shorter than he remembered at Tewkesbury, but the red glints still shone among the brown locks. He had broadened, though he was still smaller and

46

slimmer than his magnificent brother the King. Lines of tension had eased on the clever, serious face. The man seemed happier, more content, though those grey-green eyes were as searching as ever.

Beaumont put down the goblet murmuring his thanks. 'You wish to know my business at the Tower, my Lord. I assure you I meant no harm to the King and Sir John Gaveston should not be blamed for admitting me. I swore by all he held holy, I would do no wrong.'

'Yes, involving Gaveston was a mistake. It could have cost him his head.'

'My Lord—'

Gloucester cut off his assurances with a wave of one hand. 'I believe you. I *know* why you visited the Tower, Sir Charles, to do what *I* did, to see for yourself that all was well with my brother's children.'

Beaumont drew a breath of relief. His anxiety was now eased concerning his friend.

'And how did you find them, Sir Charles?' The question was sharp and Beaumont bit his lip reflectively before replying.

'They are attractive children, as one might have supposed. The Lady Margaret will be a beauty.'

'And The Earl of Warwick?'

'He is still very young, Sir.'

'He is backward, Sir Charles, one might almost say slow-witted.'

47

Beaumont flushed and avoided the Duke's eyes. 'Likely so, my Lord. I have little knowledge of children at such a tender age.'

'But I have. Edward's Ned and Richard are lively and as disobedient as is normal enough. My own Edward is but little younger than George's son, and delicate like his mother but he can write his letters, sit his horse and is years in advance of little Warwick. No, the boy gives me cause for concern. So much so that I asked leave to take him and Margaret back with me to Middleham, but the King has seen fit to give him into Dorset's charge for the present. Later, perhaps, the children may come to stay with us.' He smiled and leaned forward a little, staring into Beaumont's face. 'You mistrust my motives?'

'Not I, my Lord.'

'But you think it strange that despite our differences I should feel affection for my brother's children?'

Beaumont drew back apace. For once he was embarrassed by the Duke's direct approach. 'His Grace of Clarence was kind to me, Sir. I had cause to love him.'

'And I did not? True enough. George was— difficult.' He paused before the final word, 'but blood is blood. He *was* my brother. The children are orphaned and need an eye to be kept on their state. However, I sent for you on another matter.'

'Sir?' Beaumont's mouth went suddenly dry.

48

'The King required to be reminded of your service to the Yorkist cause at Barnet and at Tewkesbury. That stupid quarrel between you and Sir Piers Langham was resolved long ago. Sir Piers, I am sure, would wish me to request your release. You are free to go, Sir Charles. The King rescinds his sentence of banishment. You may leave the country as you please or remain in England if you prefer to do so. Since your estate was confiscated I imagine you will continue to serve as a hired officer.'

Beaumont leaned forward and fingered the roll of parchment the Duke had placed before him. It was difficult to believe his good fortune. At last he said hesitantly, 'You have my undying gratitude, Your Grace. I had not looked for such favour at your hands.'

Gloucester gave him that rare smile, known only to his intimates. He had not the easy charm of the King, but known friends loved him with real devotion and appreciated those few glimpses of his pleasure.

'My Duchess is well and happy, Sir Charles. Holy church forbids us to hold undue malice.'

Beaumont's haughty features reddened. Again he felt himself bereft of the wit to speak his feelings aloud. 'I heard Sir Piers and Lady Alicia have been blessed with two fine children.'

'Aye, I miss Piers. There has been disagreement over the management of his estates. I have given him leave to spend some

49

time there until matters are concluded satisfactorily.' He frowned. 'Your head needs attention.'

'No, sir.' Beaumont rose, anxious to avoid undue fuss. He wished nothing now to delay his return to Margaret at 'The Golden Cockerel'. He turned and cleared his throat awkwardly. 'Do you return soon to Middleham, sir?'

'Tomorrow, why do you ask?'

'I wonder if I might request yet another favour.'

'Try me.'

'There is a girl at "The Golden Cockerel" who is under my protection.' Again he coloured. Gloucester was faintly amused.

Beaumont was greatly changed from the days when he'd stalked arrogantly through the court. Naught then would have disturbed his equanimity. He was broader, though still handsome. Those aquiline features with the bright blue eyes and that wealth of golden hair, less well kept now, but curling to the shoulders, would still make him the darling of the ladies, but he bore the signs of adversity. The skin was weather-beaten, the hands roughened. His clothes were well cut but shabby. The air of quiet efficiency heightened rather than lessened his attractions. The man was prouder if anything, despite straitened circumstances, yet he was disturbed for a lady. The matter would invite curiosity.

50

'Indeed?'

'It's not what you think.' Beaumont gave a short laugh. 'She's not yet fourteen, scarcely more than a child. Her step-father ill-used her and I brought her to London to look for employment. The girl is merchant stock, no lady.' The blue eyes challenged Gloucester to read aught into the affair. 'London is no place for such a maid. If the Duchess has a place in her household—the girl has knowledge of materials. I understand her father was a cloth merchant.'

'I am sure The Lady Anne would welcome her at Middleham. The air is bracing there but healthy. Present yourself with the girl later today at Baynards Castle. I stay there with my mother. If the girl agrees, I will take her north tomorrow.'

Beaumont stooped over the lean brown hand the Duke extended. 'You relieve me of all my anxieties, Your Grace. I could not fear for Margaret under The Lady Anne's gentle guidance.'

'Good, then you may go, Sir Charles. Have dinner at Baynards Castle then look for me afterwards.'

Beaumont withdrew bowing low. Outside the lieutenant's lodging the world seemed unbelievably beautiful. The wintry sun illuminated the grey world and shone on the raven's glossy coat, making Beaumont smile at his reflections of yesterday. He was free to

51

come or go as he pleased. No longer was there need to skulk in some inn or alley, apprehensive of possible arrest. He would take Margaret walking near the river and buy her one more parting gift. The kerchief had become sadly crumpled where he'd thrust it into the neck of his doublet. Yes, one more gift, then he'd present her to Gloucester at Baynards Castle. It would be good to catch a glimpse of friends again, then his empty purse would force him to Dover. Burgundy had need of mercenaries and paid tolerably well. Margaret Woollat would be amply provided for, this surely now was his last concern.

CHAPTER FIVE

Margaret was seated near the upstairs window overlooking the courtyard of the inn. She jumped up at once when she saw him and he laughed to see her almost fall down the stairs in her haste to greet him as he entered the tap-room.

'Where have you been? I have been half out of my mind with worry and Jake Garnet has shown his anxiety.' She stopped and stared up at him, her hand flying to her mouth, a gesture characteristic with her when surprised or nervous. 'You are hurt? How bad is it—?'

'Hush, mistress,' he said, placing his palm

gently across her mouth and with his other hand, taking her right one in a firm grasp. 'It's little enough. A knock on the head. It oozed blood a trifle. I've a hard skull. There's no harm done.'

'You must come and have it attended to.' She steered him towards the stairs, no whit of her concern diminished despite his cheerful demeanour.

'Aye, sir, come into the parlour. It's a rare cut.' Jake Garnet loomed in the doorway. 'I take it you were attacked?'

'By the King's men. I was detained over-night in the Tower.'

'And you escaped? Every moment you stay here endangers you further.' Margaret's agitation increased a hundred-fold.

'Nay, lass,' Beaumont said good-humouredly. 'I'd have had a hard task to get free from the Tower. I was released.' He allowed himself to be led into the back parlour and Bess, the innkeeper's comely married daughter, brought warm water, clean linen and salve to treat his injury. While the women fussed over him he related his experience.

'So Gloucester pleaded your cause. You were fortunate, Sir Charles. The King trusts no one as he does his brother, Lord Constable of England. You lie deeply in his debt.'

'I do that.' Beaumont nodded and sat back comfortably at last in a high backed chair and tackled with relish the meal of new baked bread and meats Bess was quick to set before him. 'That is not the end of his generosity. He has offered to take you into his service, Margaret. It will be a great opportunity and I shall feel less anxious about you, when you are out of London.'

She was very quiet and when they were alone together, she said, 'I do not think I wish to go so far to Yorkshire and among The Great Ones of the land, sir. I should not know how to behave.'

He laughed and pulled her on to his knee as he might have done the little Lady Margaret. 'Nonsense, you will soon learn. The Lady Anne, Duchess of Gloucester, is kind and good. You could not have a more considerate and accommodating mistress. I insist that you go.'

She attempted to pull away from him sulkily. 'You have no right to compel me, Sir Charles. I am not your bondswoman.'

'Of course not.' He tilted her chin towards him so that she was forced to look into his eyes. 'Be sensible, Meg. In Gloucester's household you would be safe. Have you thought your step-father might come to London and search, then claim rights over you.'

Alarm crept to her eyes. She shook her head and he ran his hand down her thick brown hair. 'Tonight I take you to Baynard's Castle and present you. I am so ordered.'

Still she was apprehensive. 'There is talk that

54

the Duke is cursed of God. Is he not crook-backed and a cripple?'

'If he were indeed so would not that invite your pity, my gentle Margaret?'

She looked shame-faced at his chiding and he continued, 'You will see he limps slightly and his shoulder was dislocated as a child. I believe this was due to some riding accident. He is as fine a man as I or Jake. You will see that for yourself tonight.'

'*Must* I go?' The question was whispered.

'I cannot force your compliance, Margaret. You will please me well if you do so.'

Her lips broke from their sulky downward droop to smile at him and he set her down on the floor with a playful slap on her rump. 'Come, let us out and see the sights, and if you are good, we will visit the shops.'

Her cry of delight was as natural as a child's. He ran to his chamber to set his appearance to rights before proceeding with the afternoon's walk.

She appeared shyer than he could have thought possible that night when he led her by the hand into the hall at Baynards Castle. He smiled as her hand clutched tightly at his and he shook his head at her. He had forgotten that never before had she been present at such a gathering. Servants scurried from table to door over-burdened with gold and silver dishes and cursing the dogs which fought over the bones and scraps in the rushes. Beaumont was forced to pull Margaret aside from the progress of one serving man who grandly bore the boar's head to the high table. That worthy allowed no man to hinder him in passing.

Gloucester sat on his mother's right hand under a canopy of cloth of silver. Cecily Neville, proud Cis, was as straight-backed and unyielding as ever. Clad from head to foot in mourning, which she had donned after her husband's death at Wakefield and seldom put aside, she made a commanding figure. It was rarely that she dined now in the hall, preferring to keep to her own apartments, but today it was clear she was enjoying the company of her youngest surviving child, some said her favourite, since he most resembled his father, the ill-fated Duke of York. He was entertaining her with some amusing tale since, even from this distance, Beaumont could see she was laughing. He looked round for companions and grinned to see Sir John Gaveston rise from his position half way down the long centre table. He came to his friend and grasped his hand warmly.

'I was told of your pardon. My felicitations. You will sit with us? I received Gloucester's invitation to dine here this afternoon.'

Beaumont looked down at Margaret Woollat's bewildered brown eyes. She was dressed in her best kirtle of russet brown with the new kerchief, freshly pressed by Bess, resplendent round her shoulders and across her youthful breasts. It was pinned in place by his parting gift, a brooch of silver gilt, which she had received from his hands, tears half of joy, half of sadness, dripping on to her gown. His own doublet, brushed and smoothed, bore the marks of his recent encounter. One tear on the left shoulder had been skilfully repaired by Bess, but he was in no attire to sit with former court companions. He declined Gaveston's invitation and after talking for a few moments on what had passed since their meeting yesterday morning, Gaveston retired to his place, promising to keep Beaumont informed about the royal children whenever he could, and Beaumont led Margaret to a bench at the foot of the table.

She ate little though he plied her with rich morsels. She was too excited. Her eyes roamed everywhere from the tapestries on the walls to the men-at-arms, the white boar displayed on their liveries, and again to the high gallery above where the minstrels played and to the ladies and gentlemen above the salt, resplendent in silks and furs, the head-dresses of the women towering above the heads of their escorts. Her own simple coif and hood of white linen seemed so out of place, here. From time to time he whispered in her ear and pointed out those of importance he recognised.

'On the Duke's left, Sir Francis Lovell, his dearest friend and by him, Sir Richard Ratcliffe, another favoured gentleman. The lady in black is the Queen's and the Duke's mother, the widowed Duchess of York. The Lady Anne's mother, the Countess of Warwick, lives with them at Middleham. You will see much of her.'

'I shall not know what to do among these grand folk, truly, sir.'

He ignored her frantic comment and gave his attention to the food before him. He'd had little opportunity recently to fare so well without dire forebodings about his ability to pay his reckoning. He judged Gloucester had recognised the fact and issued the invitation with that purpose in mind. He took full advantage. He was sharp-set, having been starved of food yesterday during his sojourn in the Tower.

After the meal the Duchess withdrew to her apartments on the arm of her son. Beaumont set himself to wait in patience until he was sent for. He felt Margaret trembling throughout her body as he led her into the Duke's chamber when the summons came.

She curtseyed low, as he had tutored her, and the Duke bade her rise in his quiet, courteous manner.

'So you are the maiden who is to enter my wife's service.'

'If it pleases you, your Grace.' She nervously twisted her hands in an agony of shyness.

'It does please me since Sir Charles tells me you are an efficient and industrious worker.

You will like Middleham, I think. The gardens will soon bloom in the Spring and the dales are lovely in Summer. You will not find my Duchess a hard taskmistress, do not fear.'

She bowed her brown head, close to tears. The Duke looked over her head at Beaumont's tall form and then indicated a seat near the window. 'Sir over there, mistress, while I speak with Sir Charles.'

She went obediently. A large hound with greying muzzle padded close and she fondled its ears gently. It stretched out near her, obviously used to demonstrations of affection.

'You need have no further fears for her.' Gloucester smiled his lips twitching with mischief. 'She is younger than I expected.'

Beaumont's blue eyes flashed fire at the other's implied teasing. 'I swear she is untouched. I pray she will stay unmolested.'

'She has rare affection for you.'

'She trusts me as an elder brother.'

'Think you so?' The Duke's question was dry. 'Well, let that be. How say you, Sir Charles, to accompanying her?'

Beaumont's chin jerked up abruptly. 'You would have me in your service, My Lord of Gloucester?'

'I never waste time in senseless talk. Aye, will you serve me?'

'There is naught I would rather do but—'

Gloucester's eyebrow arched upwards. 'No buts. Loyal service or nothing. Has any other call on you?'

'No. I have no service with Charles of Burgundy. I was hired for seasons only. I owe no allegiance.'

'Then you need to attach yourself to some great house. Forgive me if I note your apparel. Your purse is slender, Sir Charles. It needs refilling. As I mentioned, I miss Piers Langham. The King has made me Warden of the Marches and Guardian of the Border. I see possible future action in Scotland. I need experienced men of my household. You served my brother loyally. I see no reason why you should not transfer that allegiance to me.' He turned to the window. 'It will reassure the little maid.'

Beaumont dropped gracefully to one knee. 'I accept service with you, My Lord. I swear now to hold no man's cause before yours. My sword will be yours alone. Since you place new trust in me, you will not find me wanting.'

The Duke inclined one lean brown hand and Beaumont kissed it. 'So be it. Sir Piers will be surprised to find you installed at Middleham when he rejoins me after his stay in Kent. You'll find Lady Alicia vastly changed, but as lovely as ever.'

It was with mixed feelings that Beaumont returned to 'The Golden Cockerel' with Margaret Woollat. His visit to London had strange repercussions, not what he had hoped, but he was by no means dissatisfied.

Margaret was enthralled by the journey north. She sat behind Beaumont, her hands clutching him so tightly round the waist, that he felt her excitement at each new sight. The icy spell gave place to warmer weather and it was a pleasant ride. Richard travelled by easy stages, pausing for a longer stay in Nottingham and yet again in York. Margaret shivered at sight of the shrivelled heads on Micklegate Bar, the grisly reminder of Wakefield and its aftermath. Here the Duke's head had been exhibited, crowned in spite by the vengeful Margaret but the Minster lifted her soul with its splendour of soaring arches. Richard heard mass and paid for requiems as his usual custom was for his father, young Rutland and now another brother, George of Clarence.

Beaumont saw little of him during the early stages but now they were in the heart of his own country, he signalled his new captain forward and pointed out his favourite landmarks as they rode. The snow was at last retreating from the hills and the dales wore the new spring grass like a festive gown. Now they glimpsed the great Abbeys, Fountains, Jervaulx and in Wensleydale itself the Grey Keep of Middleham towering over the swine market and clustering houses.

The Lady Anne with the Countess of Warwick crossed the drawbridge to greet the Duke. Beaumont did not fail to note the fervour with which he clutched his wife to his breast. A boy ran from behind, laughing and panting to be lifted high into the air by his proud father. This was the lad Gloucester had compared then to Clarence's heir. As he placed the boy on his charger, White Surrey, Beaumont saw the reason for the Duke's concern for his nephew. As he had said, the boy was small-boned and delicate like his mother but he was boisterous enough and delighted to relate his recent exploits to his amused sire. Grooms hurried to take the horses and the company began to disperse, each man about his private concerns. The family group, now entering the main courtyard, seemed to notice only each other and Beaumont stood silent, for once unsure of himself while Margaret looked bewildered and not a little afraid.

The Duke turned and called him forward. 'Sir Charles, bring Mistress Woollat.'

Margaret was inclined to hang back but Beaumont urged her forward to the two stately ladies, who seemed to her like beings from another world in their silken, fur-trimmed gowns and high hennins.

'I must disappoint you, Anne, my love, in not returning with George's children. More of that later but I bring you a new serving maid, Mistress Margaret Woollat, and I think you will remember George's former squire, Sir Charles Beaumont who joins our household.'

Not sure of his reception. Beaumont bowed low, watchful for the Duchess's reaction. He had given her ill tidings on more than one occasion. Would sadness cloud her gentle features now when she was asked to accept a man who'd proved himself her enemy? He prayed she would forgive for Margaret's sake. If she took a dislike to the child because of her association with him Margaret's stay here in the castle could bring only deep unhappiness. He need not have worried.

She held out her hand to the frightened girl. 'My husband tells me you come to serve me. We lack feminine company here at Middleham and gossip about fashion is always welcome. I hope you will not be lonely here after London.'

Margaret looked from her to the fair-haired boy who nestled against his father's side. She could not fear in this woman's company. 'I shall be very happy here in this lovely county,' she said in a sudden rush of gratitude for the Duchess's spontaneous kindness. 'I have not always lived in London. I shall not miss its dirt and plagues.'

'Nor do we, though in truth we miss the news of court sometimes.' The Lady Anne held out a small white hand to her husband's new captain.

'Sir Charles, my ladies will delight in your company, I'm sure, unless you've changed mightily from past days.'

'I think you will find I have done, your Grace,' he said quietly, stooping to press his lips to her finger tips.

Rising, he met her eyes, those unusual blue almost violet eyes, huge in the small face. There was no trace of animosity on her serene features. She looked much better than he'd dared to expect. The clean air of the North suited her and she was content. He could see that. Love gave a protective cloak to the beloved. They could afford to forgive and to live without enemies. She would always be frail. A flicker of foreboding touched him as he remembered how her sister had died in childbirth. Despite the accusation made boldly by Clarence that witchcraft had brought about her death, Beaumont could not doubt that the affliction of the lungs from which she had ever suffered had been a contributory cause. After The Lady Anne had fled from Clarence's house and been found by Gloucester, she had had a wracking cough. There were those who had seen traces of blood on her kerchief after such bouts. He feared she had inherited a family weakness. His eyes passed to the fair boy, flushed now on the cheeks with two hectic spots of red from excitement. Gloucester would be doubly bereft if the sickness should strike at his son too.

He bade farewell to the timid Margaret before she was borne away by the Duchess. Gloucester summoned his steward and bade him put an apartment at Beaumont's disposal.

'We'll meet at dinner, Sir Charles. Later I'll discuss with you some of your duties.'

Beaumont bowed respectfully. He knew Middleham from the old days when Clarence visited Warwick at his Yorkshire lair. Now he followed the steward to a room in the South Tower. It was large and well lighted. In an hour servants had kindled a fire in the grate and brought fresh linen for the bed. He would rest well here and Margaret would be safe from unwelcome attentions of her step-father, and for that matter, others who would be only too delighted to take advantage of her vulnerable position. She was such a child and had seemed even more so during the journey. Each new landscape had pleased her and among those nobles she had shown her timidity. Yes, it was worth a great deal to be home again. He could keep a watchful eye on the child. He went to the window and peered over the dale across the moat. Reflectively he stroked his chin. Assuredly he would do well to serve Gloucester loyally. The man had surprised him. It was clear that here, in the North, he was immensely popular. York had shown its approval by the acclaims of the citizens. The King was indeed fortunate that his brother's motto bore the words 'Loyalty bindeth me'.

PART TWO

Autumn 1482 to Summer 1483

CHAPTER SIX

Beaumont rode into Middleham in the late afternoon. He was surprised to find the courtyard almost deserted. Sleepy grooms came up to take charge of the mounts. He dismissed the company and turned to his quarters. The ostler smiled as Beaumont stroked the horse's satiny coat with a gentle hand.

'I rode him hard so we would reach here before nightfall.'

'I'll treat him royally, sir. Never fear.'

'The castle is quiet this afternoon.'

'Aye, sir.' The man grinned. 'Only for a spell. There's a hawking party through the dale. Like as not the Duchess will visit the Convent. It's a while since she saw the Abbess and the princess remembers her too.'

'The princess?' Beaumont looked blank.

'The Lady Elizabeth, sir, is here with the Marquess of Dorset, her step-brother, to stay some weeks at Middleham. The hunts and banquets are in her honour.'

'I see.' Beaumont smiled. 'There seems little point in attempting to report to the Duke then at present. That's just as well. I'm bone weary.'

He left his horse in good hands and walked slowly through the courtyard to his apartment. He had grown at last wearied of the journey, splendid though it had been with the glory of autumnal tints in the falling leaves, the bright red of rowan berries and the busy gurgle of streams beginning to swell with September rains. Truth to tell October had been wonderful, the sun shining forth in fierce bounty, a farewell to the summer. The last two weeks all had enjoyed the warmth, the more so as it had been unexpected and late in coming. It was no wonder the Royal party at Middleham had taken advantage of so fine an afternoon.

His squire, young Will Rawlings, came hurriedly to help him with the harness. Afterwards he waved the boy away to rest and looked out of his chamber for a passing servant to bring refreshment. A girl heard his call and came at once from the buttery with a jug of brown ale. He downed it gratefully, and stretched himself on his bed. He had pushed the men remorselessly, determined to reach their destination instead of staying at another inn en route. The effort had been worth the discomfort for tonight they would dine in hall and feast royally, since visitors from London were to be present. His eyes closed wearily. His squire had been instructed to wake him in good time so that he might strip and sluice himself before donning the elegant clothes he had bought some months ago. They had not yet been worn. He would flaunt himself before the company in fine feathers tonight. His lips curved in a half smile. It was more than likely that Margaret Woollat would be near the Duchess's side. It was Anne's practice to treat the girl as more of a companion than a serving wench. He had not seen Meg in over two years. It would be interesting to see how she'd changed, loyal practical Meg with the wealth of nut-brown hair. He'd impress her tonight and the thought gave him unusual pleasure.

He woke abruptly, a hand stealing out for his dagger. An amused voice commented on the action.

'There lies the soldier lately come from the field. What, still wary, Charles?'

Beaumont blinked as unaccustomed light smote his eyes. He forced his lids to remain open and focused his gaze on the man who sat on a small stool by his bed and grinned down at him.

'Piers, Piers Langham.' He struggled upright, clasping his hands round his bent knee.

'He, in person. They told me you'd ridden in earlier. I was out with the hawking party. I dressed early, determined to see you before we dine.'

Beaumont laughed joyously. He reached out and grasped the other's hand and they sat there grinning inanely, their fingers clinging together while they examined each other's features for the changes the years had wrought.

Piers Langham had grown taller, broader, he was almost burly, his brown hair waved thickly back from his good-humoured face. He had certainly put on weight, but the years had been kind to him. There was no mistaking the expression of contentment. Here was a man well content with his lot.

Beaumont had not seen him since that last day in the tent, after their encounter. Whenever Langham had been in attendance in Gloucester, Beaumont had been away from Middleham on the Duke's business. Lately he had been in Berwick keeping the Duke's peace. In 1480 he'd ridden North in the Duke's train to deal with risings on the border. Gloucester had soon proved his mastery. The border was safe and in Edinburgh he had imposed his own terms. For almost two years Beaumont had remained in or near abouts Berwick. Now, at last, he'd been relieved and was glad to be home. Middleham *was* home, or so he'd come to consider it.

'All's well in Berwick?' Piers's voice carried only the faintest doubt.

'Aye, all quiet. I'll report to the Duke later.'

'He'll be glad to see you?'

'He's well?'

'In excellent health and spirits. The household is gay and in festive mood. We entertain The Lady Elizabeth.'

'So I heard.'

Piers chuckled. 'The lass seems little concerned that she is not, after all, to be Queen of France in the future. I think she is secretly

72

relieved.'

'Louis of France did ill to break faith with the King's Grace, even so. It was mortal insult to wed the Dauphin elsewhere after he was pledged to our Bess. This could have precipitated war.'

Langham shook his head. 'Edward is in no heart for war, my friend. He's content for Gloucester to keep the peace for him. We have a merchant King, it seems.'

As Will Rawlings put his head round the door and hesitated, embarrassed at sight of his master's visitor, Beaumont signalled for him to enter.

'Come in, Will. Sir Piers will excuse me if I rise now, and wash and dress. I've slept late.'

'I'll stay awhile and talk while you dress, if you give me leave.'

Charles smiled. 'Willingly, I've much to ask you. Is the Lady Alicia with you?'

'Aye.' Piers grinned. 'You'll see tonight how lovely she's grown.'

'She was always that.'

Sir Piers Langham was silent for a moment while Beaumont sluiced himself with water and rubbed himself vigorously with the rough towel his squire handed him. They were both thinking of the time they'd been rivals for Alicia Standish's hand. She was a wealthy heiress and there was no denying Beaumont had both admired the lovely girl and desired to acquire her dowry. They'd settled their differences long ago. Now they would meet in hall, Lady Alicia and Beaumont after all these years. It would prove an interesting experience.

'The children are at home. The boy needs the firm hand of his tutor. We shall return for Christmas.'

'How is the Lady Anne?' Beaumont adjusted a gold and enamel chain over his new blue velvet doublet. He stared grimly at his reflection in the mirror. The cut of the doublet was not as fine as he could have wished but it fitted well. The cloth was good. No York tailor could be expected to have the skill and flair of a London one, but the garment became him. His hair had been raggedly cut while on active service but it would grow. He caught his friend's amused expression in the glass. The mirror was an expensive luxury, one of the first he'd permitted himself after earning his first crowns in the Duke's service. It had been bought from a pedlar, was decidedly Italian, though not of finest Venetian quality. There were flaws in the glass but it served his purpose and he'd had it mounted on wood for extra convenience. He frowned at Langham's grin.

'It's clear you are as vain as ever, Charles.'

'I've had little opportunity to bedeck my person. Is it so strange I should wish to look my best for the first time I am present in a civilised community?' His reply was sharp.

Sir Piers shrugged. 'No cause for heat, my friend. I but tease you. You are as elegant as ever. I simply ask myself for whose bright eyes do you array yourself so finely.'

Angry colour stained Beaumont's cheeks and the other dug him genially in the ribs. 'You're still hot of temper, Charles. I mean no harm. Come down now. Supper will soon be served. Alicia waits to see you.' He took his friend's arm as they left the chamber, and later crossed the courtyard for the main hall. 'You asked after the Duchess? I confess I've never seen her in better spirits. She seems much improved which is lucky since I know Richard is concerned that she shall not overtire herself while The Lady Elizabeth is here.'

The atmosphere in The Great Hall was one of merriment. Laughter echoed across its width as the sweating servitors rushed around trying not to slip on the rushes in their haste to present their choice dishes to the company. Sir Piers made for the high table where Gloucester sat at ease, his Duchess on his right and his distinguished niece on his left.

Beaumont bowed gracefully and was well received.

'Welcome home, Sir Charles. I hear you have been home some hours.'

'All is well in Berwick, sir, and like to remain so. You were not in the castle. Since my report is not urgent, I did not seek to importune you, when you were likely to be engaged in other matters.'

'I am pleased to hear your good news. Lady

Elizabeth, may I present to you one of my gentlemen, Sir Charles Beaumont.'

The princess had none of her mother's languid affectation of manners. She was a true Plantagenet with the pink and white complexion and clear blue eyes of her father. Her hair was hidden from sight, true to fashion under her hennin but Beaumont judged it was thick and fair as the women of the family seemed all to have in common. Her eyes danced as she charmingly bade him welcome and turned to her handsome half-brother at her side. Dorset was the true dandy. He had inherited his mother's fairness and her sophisticated air of boredom. He was elegantly dressed in a black velvet doublet, slashed with white and gold. He regarded Beaumont with only scant attention, his eyes moving away as if in search of some fresh beauty to liven his jaded palate. Beaumont was about to take his leave and seek his place at table when his eyes caught and held those of the stately dame on the Duchess's left.

She held her head regally, as she always had. Resplendent in rich wine-coloured brocade, Lady Alicia Langham put all other women to shame in the crowded hall. Long, dark lashes swept back as their owner flashed dark eyes at him and he bowed low, for a moment almost bereft of speech. She had matured splendidly. Like her Lord, she was superbly happy. It was apparent in the carriage of her lovely head. She was proud of her beauty and content with her lot. Unlike Piers she had remained as slim and dainty as ever and as mischievous.

'I see you remember me, sir.' The corners of her mouth quirked becomingly.

'I shall never forget I had the honour once to be betrothed to you, lady.'

One eyebrow was raised as if in challenge, then she nodded charmingly.

'Now that I am a staid housewife you will be circumspect, sir.'

'I must, lady.' He curled his lip in a half-smile, 'else your Lord would put a poniard between my ribs.'

'He might at that.' She turned to Piers who smiled at her good-humouredly. 'Yet he will grant us leave to talk of old times later this evening.'

Again Beaumont bowed low. 'It will be my pleasure, madam.'

She dismissed him with a nod. He smiled up at the Duchess of Gloucester, who inclined her head gently, then he moved away with Sir Piers Langham.

Throughout the meal Sir Piers regaled him with knowledge of court and castle. Beaumont only half listened. He was bemused by Alicia Langham's beauty. She had been a child so long ago and he had been interested only in her inheritance, now she bewitched his senses. It was some time since a woman had so stirred him. There had been wenches in Berwick, attentive and willing, but his proud soul had sickened at their innate coarseness. He moved irritably, knocking his wine cup from the table and spilling some on to his fine woollen hose. He gave a muttered curse, excused himself to Sir Piers and left the hall.

The courtyard was bright with flaring torchlight, almost deserted and still surprisingly warm for autumn. He was grateful for the quietness and stood, his back to the grey stone wall, staring across to the black arch of the gatehouse. He was angry with his own depression of spirit. Middleham had meant warmth and gaiety to him, during the hardships of the journey. He had looked eagerly for a welcome from Meg.

He frowned. Why, he had forgotten the child. His first sight of Alicia had wiped all thought of her from his mind. Alicia had brought back memories, hopes, ambitions. He narrowed his blue eyes to mere slits. God's pox on the fortunes of war. He had planned carefully and had stood to gain by Clarence's favour whichever rose bloomed in England. Alicia Standish would have furnished his coffers. He had not cared then if she had been plain or fair of face. Now she was wife to Piers Langham. Beaumont did not deceive himself that his present emotions were the first stirrings of illicit love. He *could* have enjoyed the lady. To attempt to woo her now would mean death to his hopes. No, she was not for him. It was merely that sight of her had aroused in him the old discontent; the knowledge that his was not a name or fortune to offer any woman of birth. Gloucester had treated him generously. He would serve The Duke loyally. There was no question of that, but Gloucester's ambitions did not rise high as Clarence's had done. Gloucester worshipped his elder brother, the sun-crowned Edward. Yet Sir Piers had hinted that Edward's star had begun to wane. He had been ill recently, grown fat, taken little exercise, despised the war-like enterprises which had formerly made his name ring from shore to shore of Britain. And if England were like to die, who would stand between those tender sons of his and the ravaging wolves which waited on the fringe of every court? The Lady Elizabeth had shown no sign of anxiety, but Elizabeth was young. She saw no fear of death. As yet it had not touched her as it shadowed her younger cousins in the Tower, Clarence's children. Beaumont fingered the hilt of his dagger moodily. What ailed him that he stood alone, while the company roistered in the hall behind him? He had expected a gayer homecoming.

As he turned back into the castle, his way was blocked by an elegant young woman, presumably a lady-in-waiting of the Princess Elizabeth. He bowed and made to pass by her, but she called him back by name.

'I was in search of you, Sir Charles.'

Her voice was familiar. He turned slowly to take in the sober but elegant kirtle of golden brown brocade over an under-robe of darker brown, her high hennin edged with dark-brown velvet framing a serious but pleasing countenance. Just now the brows were contracted in a frown of annoyance and the lips tense, but undoubtedly it was a comely face. His own lips parted in a smile of incredulity.

'Meg, Meg Woollat.'

She gave no answering smile and her tone was cool. 'The Duchess requests your attendance later in her chamber, sir. She wishes to thank you for the hour book you sent her from Edinburgh.'

'I didn't recognise you in that gown.'

'You didn't *notice* me.' He ignored the increasing chill in her manner.

'So you *did* get the gifts, I am glad of that.'

'The gold chain is very fine, sir. You should not have spent so much on a gift for me.'

'Meg,' he grimaced at her formal tone, 'did you like the chain?'

'I have said it is very fine. I am grateful.'

He was aware now of the reason for her coldness. He cursed his stupidity. He had meant to look for her when he entered the hall. Langham had steered him towards Gloucester and sight of Alicia had caused him to overlook Margaret's presence. She was piqued. That was natural enough. She had always looked eagerly for his return. He had in his baggage another gift for her, a length of green silk he had bought from a merchant captain in Edinburgh. He had chosen it with Meg in mind. It would complement her dark eyes and the rich brown of her hair. He frowned as he noted she had hidden all trace of it beneath the steeple head-dress, but her eyebrows were not shaved in the new fashion. He was glad of that. Meg's eyebrows expressed fiercely each and every emotion. He would have regretted their loss. He laughed suddenly. He would not stand this nonsense, not from his Margaret. Stooping, he seized her by the shoulders and planted a kiss on her cheek.

She withdrew herself from his embrace, tilting her chin obstinately. Her cheeks flushed with anger, though she did not punish him as any other maid might with a stinging slap. He fell back apace, his face thoughtful. Indeed he might have preferred an impulsive blow. This cool resentment was unlooked for in the child who had ever greeted him with delight.

'Meg,' he said quietly, 'what ails you?'

'Naught ails me, Sir Charles. As you see I am perfectly well.'

'In what way have I angered you?'

'Angry, sir—I?' She shook her head. 'I have no cause for anger.'

He did not press his point. Tomorrow he would tease her from her jealous mood. She would be again his fresh, unspoilt Margaret.

He would chase her on the green until she was spent with laughter and she would fall exhausted into his arms as she had so many times. Now he would play her game. She had become the stately dame and he would treat her as such. He bowed gravely.

'I will present myself at her Grace's apartments.'

Along the corridor came the swish of silken skirts and Alicia came towards them. Unreasonably Beaumont was irritated by her appearance at this moment but was gallantly determined to conceal his embarrassment.

'Well met, Sir Charles. The Lady Anne was asking for you. Accompany me to her chamber and I'll tell you of my two treasures. I'll warrant Piers has not mentioned them. He thinks of nothing but Court affairs or the managing of the estate. I pray you have not yet dulled your wits. Your conversation was once most entertaining. Let me see if it has deteriorated.'

Beaumont flashed a final glance of appeal at Margaret. She regarded him steadily. Helpless to resist, he allowed Alicia to chatter on about Kent, her estates, the price of jewellery and the need for wit in discussion as she placed one slender hand on his sleeve and he led her towards the Duchess's apartments.

CHAPTER SEVEN

Gloucester summoned Beaumont early to his apartment and kept him there some two hours questioning him about affairs in Berwick and it was impossible for him to seek Margaret as he had hoped. Left to his own devices he sought her in her usual haunts. In the morning The Lady Anne spent an hour with her son, reading to him or listening to his repetition of his catechism, so Margaret was free then. If the day was fine she sat in the courtyard or on the green with the other maids watching the tilting or once or twice he had found her on the battlements of the North Tower, staring down across the little market town of Middleham, to the hills and dales beyond. Today she was in neither place and he hesitated. In the old days he would have gone to her chamber, now he paused. Yesterday she had seemed so grand a dame. Such a course was no longer suitable. He could not speak to her there without the presence of a third person to make the occasion seemly. He strolled over to the green to watch the young squires at the quintain. Sooner or later she would join the other young women of the household and he could proffer his gift to her then. The silk was so fine that he had folded it flat and it lay now in the leather purse suspended from his belt.

The exercises were concluded as it grew near to noon and the little group of squires and spectators broke up in search of cold meat and ale from the buttery. Still there was no sign of Margaret. Beaumont lingered on the green but in the end followed the others. She did not dine in hall and when he looked for her later in the kitchen, the servants had no news to give him. Where could the wench be? He strolled later to The Lady Anne's apartments. The Lady Anne had the young Edward with her. Beaumont excused his intrusion and asked after Margaret.

'I have a gift for Mistress Woollat,' he said awkwardly. 'There was little time to speak with her yesterday.'

'She worked with me at my embroidery earlier this morning, Sir Charles. Later I believe she went walking.'

'Alone, your Grace?'

'Oh, I think not. Members of the household often go into Middleham together.' She smiled confidently. 'I did not enquire too closely. Mistress Woollat can always be trusted to be sensible.'

He bowed and withdrew. The Countess of Warwick approached along the corridor. He did not linger. His former association with Clarence did not make him a favourite in that lady's eyes. She had never forgiven the Royal Duke's betrayal of her husband before Barnet.

He wandered out moodily into the

84

courtyard. He was free of duties and had expected to squire Margaret into the town. He was hurt by her neglect of him. Had she waited on the green with the others, he would quickly have found her. It had always been her custom to wait for him there. The courtyard and green were deserted now. The servants had taken the opportunity to doze, the young squires had escaped the hawk-like surveillance of their mentors. A yawning groom led out a horse towards the smith. The castle and its environs wore an air of sleepy indifference. He sauntered to the gatehouse, staring along the road towards the now empty swine market. He was beginning to yawn himself. He had slept ill last night though he was exhausted from the journey. The rest he had had during the afternoon had been short in duration. It was useless to stay here. He would see Margaret tonight, if not tomorrow. It was pointless to pursue the wench and give her ideas beyond her station.

He stiffened suddenly as two figures approached from the meadows. The light, high giggle was from one of the maids, but the stance of the man, even from this distance as he stooped to assist his companion over the stile, was unmistakable. Dorset, true to his reputation, had been dallying with some wench of the household. God give the girl sense. Surely here in this castle of the north, the silly chit knew of Dorset's preoccupation with the fair sex. She was hopping now along the cobbled road, and leaning upon his shoulder. Apparently she had twisted her ankle or lost a shoe. Since she was laughing gaily enough she could not be unduly hurt. He turned away, unwilling to pry on the Marquess's private concerns, then sudden anger left him ice cool and held him dead in his tracks. They were nearer now. The voice was clearer, and undoubtedly Margaret's.

'My Lord, I beg you to leave me now. I can hop the rest of the way. I am not in pain I assure you.'

There was no lack of interest now in the pleasant young voice. 'Sweet Margaret, would you have me play the knave? Let me carry you to your chamber.'

She gave a little squeal. 'Indeed no, the Duchess would be gravely disturbed. As it is I have been absent too long and must offer my excuses.'

She stopped abruptly as she caught sight of Beaumont by the gatehouse, put her foot down suddenly, gave a sharp cry of pain and staggered. Dorset steadied her expertly and eyed Beaumont insolently.

'What is it, Sir Charles? You bar our way, man. Can you not see the lady is hurt?'

Beaumont gave Margaret one smouldering look of fury and turned away. Behind him he heard her quickly muttered leave-taking then she half-stumbled, half-hopped the rest of the way to her room. He made no effort to help her but hurried to his own apartment, slammed the door and threw himself angrily on to the bed.

He seethed with fury. Dorset of all men! She could not plead ignorance of the man's nature. She had been in the Royal household long enough now to know the man's lechery was a byword. His adventures vied in entertainment with the tales of the King's own amorous intrigues. That she had been fool enough to allow such a man to accompany her to the town, filled him with disgust. He'd have no more to do with the wench. Had he protected her, provided her safe employment for this? When his fury cooled he lay in the lengthening shadows of the chamber and thought clearly of Margaret. Why had he not had eyes yesterday? She was no longer a child. Dorset had recognised her budding loveliness, and he had no shortage of feminine admirers. He, Charles Beaumont, had allowed other considerations to cloud his vision. He pictured her now as he'd seen her last night, tall and full bosomed. The shape of her face had become more defined, less broad, less blurred by youthful plumpness. Her poise had been that of a mature woman. Had he been less bedazzled by the sight of his former betrothed, he would have noted more clearly the changes two years of absence had brought about in her.

He dressed thoughtfully when Rawlings, his squire, presented himself. It was clear he must treat Margaret more carefully. She was nearing seventeen if not past that year. She needed a husband, some sensible young man who would care for her, give her children of her own, occupy her mind with the matronly pursuits which kept comely young women from mischief. He would ask Gloucester for advice. He had some income. He was willing enough to provide a small dowry for Margaret. It would suffice if the right man could be found.

He took his seat by her side in the hall. She made room for him without argument but he did not fail to note her heightened colour. Later would be a time for reckoning. She lingered at the table, stuffing herself with candied fruit, nuts and marchpane. He waited grimly not to be out-manoeuvred by so obvious a childish trick.

At last he said, 'Does your ankle pain you, mistress?'

'No, sir.' Her words were civil enough, but her eyes were stormy.

He jerked her unceremoniously to her feet and despite her brave words, tears sprang to her eyes at the jarring pain.

'Then we will talk outside, awhile.'

'It would not be seemly, sir, for me to go with you out of the hall. The Duchess would disapprove.'

He stared at her set little face, made small by the towering height of her hennin.

'If you trusted yourself in Middleham with

My Lord Marquess of Dorset, I hardly feel you are like to be in peril in my company just outside the door.'

She lowered her lashes to hide the pain of his angry words, then came with him obediently into the corridor. Looking down he saw her wincing from the pain and his irritation melted somewhat. He assisted her to a bench where visitors sometimes sat when waiting to see The Duke. She drew a long breath of relief and he realised the foot pained her more than she would admit.

'Tell me,' he said shortly, 'where did you go with Dorset?'

'It is none of your concern—'

'It *is* my concern, mistress. Argue with me and I will convince you of my interest.'

She bit her lip and turned her face from him.

'Meg,' he said more gently, 'what is this with you? The man's a known lecher. Have the sense you were born with.'

'I did not go with him alone. There were several of us, pages, serving maids and the like. We went to buy sweetmeats, then my sole broke. I could not keep up with the rest.' Her face was still turned from him but he could hear now the faint huskiness of unshed tears. 'I turned my ankle. The others had gone on. He stayed with me. I could not refuse his help. It seemed such a long way. He said there was a quicker way through the water meadows. I made excuses. I would not go with him there, only at the last, we cut through from the market. I think he was angry for he had to half-carry me and you know I am no light weight, but he was very kind and—' she gulped and pressed on, 'after all I am no more than a servant. He *did* stay and he did help me. Would you have done as much, Sir Charles?'

He was determined not to laugh now at her woeful tale. It had its comic side, true enough. He pitied Dorset's ungainly progress through the town with a weighty girl who refused to trust herself with him on the meadow path, and yet whom he could not ungallantly leave to make her way back to the castle unaided. The Marquess could not have been in the best of tempers. It was hardly possible to make lover-like suggestions to a girl who was obviously in pain and distress. Yet despite his annoyance he had shown no sign of his pique when he brought her home. Poor Meg. Her giggles had been more to hide her discomfiture than her delight in Dorset's company.

He stooped down and held out his arms. 'Come Meg, let us to go your chamber. Your foot is paining you. It must be rested. I will carry you.'

'Oh no—'

'Will you still argue, wench. Come!'

She nestled back against his shoulder as he carried her through the corridor and up the steep stone stair to her own small chamber. It was scarcely more than an alcove but it was curtained off from prying eyes and he placed her down gently on the hard little bed and sank down by her side.

'Now you are my sensible girl again, I can show you what I brought you from Edinburgh.'

She exclaimed at the bright silk, fingered it delightedly and threw her arms tightly round his neck in an access of childish devotion.

He laughed at the simple joy of holding her close in the old way. She was his little Meg again. There was no need to fear. She had not altered, grown beyond his reach. Yet even as her wet cheek nuzzled against his shoulder, he knew he was deceiving himself. This was no child in his arms. As if she sensed his thought her arms tightened round his neck, she gave a little sob and turned her face towards his. She was half lying in his arms now, the long slender column of her throat arching backwards while her eyes closed and her soft mouth was partly open for his kiss. One arm had relaxed and her fingers stole down his shoulder and arm. He waited for no more but bent and kissed her full on the mouth. She did not respond as an experienced woman might have done but she made no attempt to draw away. She gave a little sigh of satisfaction and he noted the tears still smudging her cheek. Even this could not mar her loveliness. She was wholly desirable in her youth and freshness. He kissed her more gently this time and her eyes flickered open as she stared up at him, her lips curving into a smile. As his own face remained grave, her eyes widened and she said, 'What is it? You are not angry with me. Please, say you are not still angry about the Marquess. I swear—'

He placed a gentle hand across her mouth silencing her protestations. 'Child, no. You have done nothing to anger me. I am furious with myself.'

'Because you kissed me?' Her eyes were accusing him and he drew her close again, cradling her against his shoulder.

'Because for a moment I almost did more, my Meg. You are so lovely that I forgot—'

'That I am only a serving wench.' Her voice was so harsh that for a second he hardly recognised it as hers.

'I forgot you are a child, fresh, unspoilt.'

'I am no longer a child, Sir Charles. You are a fool if you think it.'

He was silent and as her angry little face challenged him to reply he said quietly, 'As you say, Meg. I am a fool if I think that. Two years was long to be away. You are a woman and very desirable.'

'But not to you?'

'To me, Meg, and all men.'

Her lower lip drooped in a pout. 'Once before you said I was inexperienced, that you did not want me. Is that true, here and now?'

He sat up and she withdrew from him. He could see now that she was roused and angry.

If he thought to placate her with some trite phrase, he would lose the game. He tightened his own lips and looked back at her steadily, his blue eyes now hard and cold.

'I want you, but I'll not take you.'

'Because I'm a serving maid?'

'Because I respect you and I'll not spoil you, Meg.'

'Respect.' Her eyes flashed fire at him. 'What do I want with respect, Charles Beaumont? I want you to love me. Do you think I expect you to wed me? I've waited for you such a long time—' Her lips trembled but she controlled them and pressed on, 'waited and hoped for you to soon come home. Men have wanted me. Do you think you were the first to kiss me? I'd have none of them. I'm yours. I'll always be yours for as long as you want me. When you came, I heard it and I went wild with joy. I dressed with such care. When you came into the hall I—I—then you did not even *look* at me. You didn't see me. Lady Langham had all your attention. I was so hurt. I wanted to die, to creep away and hide—and—and then the Marquess asked me to go into Middleham. I thought you would be in the courtyard and see me and be angry, jealous. You weren't even there.'

'I was with Gloucester. I looked for you, Meg.'

'It doesn't matter.' Her voice was muffled now, choked with sobs. 'Nothing matters if you want me.'

'Meg, you must marry some sensible wealthy man who will protect you. I'll speak with Gloucester. There'll be a sizeable dowry. I—'

He did not finish. She withdrew from him to the bed-head and pointed one small hand at the curtain. 'Go—leave me—

'Meg.'

'Leave me.'

He gave one glance at the agony of her set little face and left her. Outside the room he turned and paused. The sound of her sobbing reached him and he hesitated, one hand on the curtain, then he descended the tower stairs. He went immediately to the stables, ordered the groom to saddle his horse and rode across the courtyard, clattered over the cobbles of the town and into the open country beyond. It was dark when exhausted, he turned for home and the torch flares from the gate-house guided him back to the castle.

During the next week Margaret avoided him. She bowed to him respectfully when he waited on the Duchess, spoke only when politeness necessitated conversation and ran hurriedly off when he approached her with the intention of attempting to explain his reasons. Only physical exertion prevented him from seeking her in her chamber, drawing her into his arms and spilling out words of mingled desire and frustration. His loins ached for her.

He was furious with his own inability to blot out of his mind his need for her. There were maids in the castle and in Middleham who were willing and able to assuage his body's ache but his mind dwelt only on Meg. In hall and courtyard his eyes sought her only. When she laughed with the squires or giggled with the maids his ears caught the sound and alerted him to her nearness. He watched Dorset like a hawk, ready for one burning glance in the girl's direction, one sign which would tell him she had succumbed to the Marquess's blandishments.

His torture was to come to an open flaring agony, the more excruciating since he was powerless to treat the cause. Ten days later The Lady Elizabeth prepared to leave her uncle's castle for London. The household was in a ferment as the trunks were packed and secured in the baggage wagons. Striding across the yard, Beaumont encountered Meg haranguing a serving man about the disposal of a large box.

'Further back, dolt. The package contains everything I own in the world also presents from the Duchess. Treat it with care.'

She turned to see Beaumont standing stock-still with astonishment. She dismissed the man and made to follow, thought better of it and said falteringly, 'I am going with the Princess. I thought you knew.'

He was silent and she flushed. 'It is best. I am

not changed, Sir Charles. I shall always love you. In London I shall not make things difficult for you and there will be no need for you to find me a husband.'

'Meg, I hurt you, I know. Let me try to explain.'

'There is no need. I understand. You are a Beaumont. I am a merchant's daughter, yet you will not let me give you my love. For some strange reason you think me too good for your mistress or is it that I am not even fit for that?'

'I will not reply to that, Meg. The suggestion is unworthy of you. I want you to have security—children.'

'I know.' She gave a little frosty smile. 'I think I *do* understand but I cannot remain here like this—wanting you. The Princess has praised my skill with the needle. She required new clothes. I asked her to take me. She was pleased to offer me a place in her household. It is not for good. The Duchess has given me leave of absence. In the spring she and the Duke travel to London. I may rejoin her household then. Our problems may be resolved. I hope so. Sir Charles, choose a gentle girl, one who will serve you well. For all your fine name, your purse remains slender. Your bride will need to be practical as well as high-born.'

He could find nothing to say. When he moved to take her hand, she backed from him, shaking her head gently.

'Meg,' he said brokenly, 'Meg—'

She smiled at him once, her chin lifting determinedly, then turned back to the disposal of the baggage.

CHAPTER EIGHT

The dark days of January infected Beaumont with a spirit of deep depression. Margaret had left Middleham and he missed her abominably. He could not have believed that it had been her presence in the castle which had previously made the place home to him. All his life he had relied on no one. His father had died soon after his birth and his mother, proud arrogant dame that she was, allowed neither of her sons to lean on her for comfort. His elder brother had inherited the small manor on the borders of Leicestershire and it had pleased Lady Beaumont that her son had been received in The Duke of Clarence's household. Her husband had fought for York at Wakefield and the younger son had been accepted as squire as a measure of payment for is father's services to the Yorkist cause. Charles had little in common with his brother, Henry, some five years his senior. He was a dour, clerkish man, well aware of a need for economy in the running of the impoverished estate. Unlike Charles he seemed unaware of the pride of ancestry which was his. A Beaumont had followed the Conqueror to England from Normandy. Charles jeered at his brother's cheese-paring ways. In Clarence's household he was determined to win prominence among the gentlemen who served the King. The turn of events had brought disaster to his hopes.

He had won Clarence's favour though none of his fellow squires had proffered him friendship. His hauteur had set him apart and his handsome fairness had won him the notice of the ladies. This also set him apart from his fellows who viewed his easy conquests with jealous dislike. In Burgundy there were high-born ladies who'd offered their hearts and sometimes their purses. He had waited to choose wisely the woman who would bear his name and give him sons. Now he knew with amazed certainty that it was the merchant's daughter, from the Chepe, whom he loved. With foolish sense of honour had kept him from accepting her love? It would be enough for Margaret were he to establish her decently. She would have his protection if not his name. He jibbed at this course, yet found it impossible to give sensible reasons. He had not feared to sire bastards with other women, had not indeed considered the matter. For Margaret he wanted only security. How could he give her that without a wedding ring and to offer his name to her was unthinkable.

Piers Langham had been a merry

companion during the days which had followed her departure in The Lady Elizabeth's train. They had hawked together, rode through the wintry Yorkshire lanes with Gloucester and the other gentlemen of the household, Sir Richard Ratcliffe and Sir Francis Lovell. Now Langham had left with his dark-eyed lady to spend Christmas on their estate in Kent and the holy season was marked with glad rejoicing at Middleham. The Duchess and young Edward seemed uncommonly well though Lady Anne confessed to Beaumont that she missed her little serving companion.

'We leave for London when the weather improves,' she said confidently. 'I hope then to encourage Meg to return to me, though London indeed offers greater attractions. It is possible she will be unwilling to leave palace service.'

Charles thought the latter suggestion very likely indeed. He sighed moodily and rode out as was his custom when attempting to raise his drooping spirits.

Middleham was well served. Now that he had been relieved from service on the border, there was little to do. Gloucester listened politely to suggestions he made for improving defences but in his own heart he knew his advice was not needed.

February passed into early March. Snow still lay thickly on the moors and dales. It was rare that the household strayed now far from town and castle. Close confinement increased Beaumont's boredom and he longed for the sun to gain strength so that training of bowmen could begin again and he could throw himself energetically into useful activity.

The Duke summoned him one morning to ride with him to Jervaulx. He had business with the Abbot but Beaumont was surprised to discover they were to ride unattended. It was a pleasant spring day and he enjoyed the exhilaration of the freshening air. When a young monk told him the Duke awaited him in the Abbot's parlour, he found Gloucester alone.

'The Abbot has provided cold meats and wine. Let us partake of his hospitality before returning. The fire is pleasant since the day is still chilly.'

Beaumont obeyed, eating well but silently. Gloucester eyed him thoughtfully. As he rinsed his fingers and dried them on a napkin thoughtfully provided by his plate, he said, 'Why so despondent, Sir Charles? Is it that your war-like nature requires action at arms to give life added zest, or is it that you miss the bright eyes of Mistress Woollat?'

Charles made no attempt at evading the question. 'It is the bright eyes of Meg Woollat I miss, your Grace.'

'You love the maid? Was she unwilling to grant you her favours?'

'Not unwilling. Indeed it was because I refused her that she left with the Princess.'

'I see.'

Beaumont played absent-mindedly with the hilt of his dagger. 'Meg is an honest woman. I would see her well bestowed with a kind husband and children round her knee. I could not give her my name.' He looked up confused, 'Your Grace must understand that.'

Gloucester nodded. 'Yes.' He moved the ring on his finger, a gesture usual with him when in deep thought. 'Yet you love the girl and she you.'

Beaumont was silent. The Duke rose and went to the window gazing out on to the cloisters where the monks walked slowly, their eyes lowered to their psalters. He said gently as if speaking to himself, 'When I fetched Anne from sanctuary, she was very ill, coughing blood. I feared for her, since the sickness was not new to her family and the misfortunes of the last months had not improved her condition. I wed her because I loved her. I shall always love her. I thought about it for a long time. It was incumbent on me to rear strong sons. I am of the blood royal. I knew well enough Anne could scarcely provide me with them. Indeed I rejoice that I have Edward, though the lad is delicate.' He paused and Beaumont did not interrupt. He stood, his brows contracted, puzzled by Gloucester's strange revealing of his innermost feelings.

'There were many who spoke openly of my lack of practical sense. The King was not silent, though he did not oppose me in the end for he knew my mind. We have each other, Sir Charles, and we are content. We both know such a state of affairs cannot endure for ever. What we have now will remain with the survivor when an end comes to our happiness.' He turned, his face was in shadow though Beaumont knew he was smiling. 'I assure you there is great comfort in that thought. Well now, we linger overlong. I have promised to visit the stables on my return. One of the mares is near to foaling and Wilkin is anxious. We must ride back before the light fades.'

Beaumont bowed as the Duke moved to the door. Gloucester placed one slender hand on his arm and gripped it. 'Come now, Sir Charles, let us see you with a smiling countenance. We need to face the spring with delight, not gloom.'

During the night Beaumont lay awake pondering the Duke's words. He recalled the careful glances Gloucester gave to his wife and child, notwithstanding his air of quiet confidence. If Anne were to die—If Meg were to die or he, Beaumont, before—A cold sweat broke out suddenly on his brow.

The next morning he requested an audience with Gloucester. He was received cheerfully.

'Your Grace, I would like leave of absence for some while. I would ride to London.'

A little smile played round Gloucester's mouth. 'I have dispatches I wish to reach His Grace the King. Tomorrow they will be ready for you and instructions also for the Minster in York. You will stay there on your ride. Await me in London if you wish. I have purchased a house there, Crosby Place. It would please me if you inspected the property to see that it is ready to receive the Duchess and household when she rides south with me as the weather improves.'

Beaumont bowed formally. 'I am at your Grace's disposal in all things, and deeply in your debt.'

CHAPTER NINE

It was late afternoon when Beaumont drew rein in the Chepe at 'The Golden Cockerel'. He was surprised to see the inn more than usually deserted. A groom took charge of his horse and he hurried into the tap-room in search of the innkeeper. He checked at the sight of two men in the Royal livery who sat in a corner drinking ale. Who in the Royal household would be likely to visit Jake Garnet's inn but Mistress Margaret Woollat? If she were indeed within, he would see her even more quickly than he had hoped. Impatient to reach her, he had pushed himself almost beyond human limit to reach London by the beginning of the month. He had been delayed some days in York on the Duke's business but it was yet only the tenth day of April. He had done well. He called for service and Bess, the innkeeper's daughter came through the back door to greet him.

Her face broke into a beaming smile of welcome as she gestured him through to the private parlour above the tap-room.

'Sir Charles, it is fortunate you arrive at this hour. Your friend Mistress Woollat is just about to leave.'

Margaret rose as they entered the room. He could see she wore an expression of unaccustomed gravity, but there was no mistaking her pleasure at seeing him. He grasped her two hands and conveyed them to his lips.

'Fortunate indeed. I would have sought you tomorrow after I presented the Duke's messages to his Grace the King.'

She lifted her face to his and he saw it strained and pale in the uncertain light from the horn windows. 'You have not heard? The King died yesterday.'

He was stunned by the tidings and repeated her words clumsily. 'The King—dead?'

'He has been ailing some months. He took to his bed this last week and died yesterday afternoon. Priests were summoned. Praise God he was in a state of grace.'

'Gloucester will have no suspicion. The court must be in a ferment.'

Margaret glanced covertly at the door. 'I came to see Jake. I often do. I have been sick for old friends. The palace is no place today to raise one's spirits. The Lady Elizabeth is closeted with her mother. I knew she could not miss me, nor will she for some time. I shall be needed to refurbish her mourning gowns, beyond that, there will be little call for a sewing maid for many months.'

Jake sighed to Bess to withdraw. 'I'll leave you to hear all the news, Sir Charles. The Duke will want all the details and from all sources. You must be tired. I'll send up supper and Bess will prepare a room.'

Beaumont nodded gratefully and stripped off his gloves. As the door closed, he said, 'Come Meg, tell me all you can. What is the state of affairs at Westminster? Is it imperative I know everything. Take your time and be thorough.'

'The King has been unwell for some weeks. Several times he has left the council chamber early and once or twice has taken to his bed. It is believed he took a severe chill. He seemed better, then suddenly yesterday his condition worsened and the Queen was sent for and the younger children. She was with him when he died.'

'Was there a council meeting?'

'Lord Hastings presided over one hastily

105

called together last evening. I understand the King's will was read. There was gossip in the court.' She shrugged. 'One expects that but it seems the Lords could not agree. As you know the young King is at Ludlow under the tutorage of his uncle.'

'Rivers. Aye, I know it. They will be sending for him to come quickly to London.'

'I think it was to make arrangements for this that the council was called.'

'Gloucester is surely named Regent for the King.'

Margaret made to say something then shook her head, her eyes betraying concern.

He settled at once on her hesitancy. 'There are suggestions to the contrary?'

She bit her lip. 'Lord Hastings was said to be angry. His voice was raised in Council. He and the Marquess of Dorset are on bad terms.' Her lips twisted wryly. 'Not that that is surprising for other reasons.'

He turned, frowning. 'Oh?'

'Mistress Shore. They have long been rivals for her affections.'

'Jane Shore? But I thought the King—'

'Oh yes, but her sidelong glances have lately been directed towards Dorset.'

'You are sure of this?'

'I have been close to The Lady Elizabeth and the Queen. I cannot fail to see what has been patently plain.'

'What's to be done, then? Have you heard?'

'Little enough. A large escort has been sent to Ludlow for the King, though smaller than originally intended. Hastings was insistent that such a force was unnecessary. He has taken it upon himself to inform The Duke of Gloucester. As Lord Chamberlain, no one could deny him that right.'

'Gloucester will ride first to York. It will be some time before he reaches London. The damage could be done by then.'

She looked blank and he made haste to reassure her. 'Soft there, Meg. I talk in riddles. These matters are no concern of yours.'

'The Queen is distraught. She weeps constantly and is in the way of the servants while they are packing her clothes and the children's.'

He caught her wrist hurriedly and she gave a little cry of pain. He muttered an apology and relaxed his grip.

'Pardon, Meg. I was startled. Did you say "packing"?'

'Yes, that is so.'

'But where should she go?'

She stared at him wide-eyed. 'I do not know, but she is in a panic. She runs from one room in the apartment to another, pulls young Richard towards her and covers him with hysterical kisses, then sits in the midst of all the disorder and dissolves again into a flood of tears.'

She broke off as Bess knocked softly and came in, on Beaumont's invitation, with a tray of meat, bread and ale. He set to, and nodded as she informed him that his room was ready, the bed well aired and his horse attended, then dropped a quick curtsy and left. Margaret shook her head at his offer of food.

'Strange behaviour,' he said at last after a long pull at the ale jack. 'I would expect the Queen to weep, poor lady, but pack—!'

'She is distraught. I don't think she knows what she is doing. Lord Dorset is always there whispering and exhorting her. One would think he was the father and she his child.'

'He was at the Council, Dorset, I mean?'

'Oh yes, he is Constable of the Tower and so his presence was essential.'

Beaumont speared beef on to his knife and regarded it thoughtfully. 'I had forgotten that factor.'

'I must return. I should not stay here, though indeed no one notes whether I come or go.'

Beaumont lowered the knife and leaned forward over the table. 'You are sure of that?'

She came back from the doorway and leaned eagerly towards him. 'Is there something you wish me to do?'

He put one finger to his mouth and bit it reflectively. 'Is there one at the Palace you could trust to carry a message to the Tower? I wish none to know I am here in London for the present. You understand?'

She nodded. 'I have made friends.'

He went to the door and called to Bess.

108

'Bring parchment, lass, if you have it, and ink and quill.' He came back to Margaret's side and drew her to him, staring intently into her eyes. She flushed but did not withdraw. 'You can trust my discretion,' she said at last quietly.

'Meg, I know that. It is your safety which concerns me.' He nodded suddenly at her expression of amazement. 'Your messenger is to seek out Sir John Gaveston and deliver my note. He will most probably be found in the Tower, where he has been recently on guard, or in the Palace. He will know then that I am here and I hope, come to me.'

'That is all?'

He reached out and placed firm hands on her shoulders. 'That is all you can do there. When you can, join me here.'

A sudden flame lit up her eyes and he stooped and kissed her gently. 'If it is still your wish, my Margaret, to trust to my protection.'

'I have not changed, nor will I do so.'

He lifted up her chin and gazed long and earnestly at her. She would never be a fashionable beauty, but there was a brooding, indefinable quality which gave strength to the young face. Saddened by the events she had witnessed at Westminster, she no longer appeared to him child-like, but a mature women, her resolution steady as a rock on the moors they both knew so well.

'There is work I must do first, Meg. I will not hide from you in facts. There will be danger, intrigue. Do you trust me to deal honourably with Gloucester?'

She gazed fearlessly back at him. 'You know that I do.'

'When Gaveston comes here we will discuss what is to be done. If you are here I may rely on your help. Later I must ride to meet the Duke.'

She drew a sudden breath and he clasped her hands tightly within his own. 'I swear we shall not long be parted. Trust me now. Wait while I write, then carry my note for me.'

When Bess came with the writing materials, Margaret sat quietly in the darkening room until Bess lit the rush-lights, then she placed the sealed parchment in the neck of her gown lifted her face for Beaumont's kiss and left him, to return to Westminster.

He finished his meal hurriedly and went immediately to his chamber. Sleep came quickly as it did when there was need for action in the future. He had trained his body to obey his will. Tomorrow he would need a clear head and an agile frame. Sleep now was a necessity.

He came down early and broke his fast in the parlour. From the window he could glimpse signs of the grief that had subdued London. Their splendid merchant King was dead. He had squandered their money, cuckolded husbands, led them to war, but he was a beloved giant, feckless, licentious but a charmer of souls and they mourned him as they thought fitting. Even the cries of the apprentices lacked their usual verve. Men went about the normal business of the day with but little enthusiasm. One could sense the tension. What now? The young Edward was ill-fitted for the mantle of sovereignty. Were they once more to be plunged into a maelstrom of intrigue, war and death? They shook their heads as they talked together in little knots by the street corners. God bring them a protector to take Edward's place. He was needed.

He leaned from the window as a man approached the inn and looked upwards at the sign. Beaumont hesitated before thrusting wide the casement and signalling to him. He drew back, watching, and drew a relieved breath as the man, obviously satisfied, passed inside the inn yard.

He rose to greet his visitor when Bess brought him up and dismissed her for ale for them both.

'God bless you, John. I feared you might fail me.'

The other drew off his gloves, hooked forward a stool and seated himself. 'What would you have me do?' he asked quietly.

'Are Clarence's children lodged in the Tower?'

'Aye, but not for much longer.'

'Dorset plans to move them?'

'He gave orders yesterday that their belongings were to be packed and the children prepared for a journey. He wishes them conveyed to a place of safety.'

'Safe for whom—the children or Dorset?'

Gaveston regarded him silently. 'You hinted before that Dorset might harm the children. I'm inclined to believe you but I see no motive.'

'He has his reasons. John, will you trust me? At present I am not willing to reveal those reasons or my fears.'

'I understand.'

'I want the children in the care of one I can trust.'

'You know of such a one?'

Beaumont nodded. 'Sir Piers Langham is on his estate in Kent. He would accept the trust I lay on him.'

'You plan to seize the children?'

'Yes.'

Gaveston pursed his lips. 'They are well guarded. Dorset is Constable of the Tower. How will you free the children from such a fortress?'

'What instructions did he give the nurse? Try to be exact. Do you know if the new guardians were mentioned by name, or described? Is there to be a warrant of proof of authority?'

Gaveston shook his head. 'That would be unlikely if—' He broke off and shrugged.

'If murder is intended, just so, my friend. The men who take charge of the children will not be named. They will fade discreetly into the background—afterwards, well paid for their services. The nurse will hand over the children

112

without too many questions. Dorset is occupied with matters of grave import. Will he have time for the children? I think not. If I were to present myself with some parchment, sealed like as not, who will look closely? The children will be entrusted to me.'

'It is ill devised, Beaumont. If Dorset were to go to the Tower or if—'

'Ifs, ifs, my friend. We must risk the consequences. We have not the time to wait for My Lord of Gloucester. I am little known at court. Dressed simply I could pass for a hired mercenary. It must serve. The plan's audacity is its only merit.'

Gaveston rose. 'You will need a closed carriage. Some woman must go with them—'

'I have such a woman.'

'Trustworthy?'

'To the death.'

'Very well, I will arrange transport, a driver and a man-at-arms to accompany you.'

'I cannot go to Kent.'

'But why?'

'I ride to join Gloucester when this is done. Where did Hastings advise the Duke to meet with the King's party? Do you know?'

'Northampton.'

'There will be time.'

Gaveston drew on his gloves and prepared to leave. 'If you think it best *I* will take young Warwick and his sister to Kent.'

'If you trust your man, I think not. Your

113

absence from your duties will excite suspicion. The longer I have to start the children on their way the better the chance of success.'

'Yes, you are right but—'

'Can you have the coach here at this inn this afternoon?'

Gaveston was startled. 'As soon as that?'

'I'll risk no delay.'

'Yes, it shall be done.' Bess entered with the ale. They broke off to drink deep and to wait till her steps died away below.

Gaveston reached out and clasped hands with his friend. 'God be with you, Charles. Take care.'

Beaumont smiled grimly. 'My head has rested firmly on my shoulders despite storms. God willing it will remain so.'

He waited until Gaveston was clear of the inn then went in search of Garnet, the innkeeper.

CHAPTER TEN

Margaret was seated in the parlour by the window when Beaumont returned to the inn later that afternoon. Her hooded cloak was neatly folded over a chair and her bundle was stowed out of the way under the table. She showed no surprise at his changed appearance.

On Jake Garnet's recommendation he had

sought a draper on London Bridge and bought from him woollen homespun hose, a shirt of coarse linen, leathern well-worn jerkin and a cloak of grey. He looked every inch the hired soldier. His fair hair had been pushed under a round, green hat and the long liripipe would serve to conceal the lower part of his features if he wished to avoid too close a scrutiny. He tossed hat and cloak on to the table, hitched up his leathern belt with its serviceable broadsword and perched on the table's edge.

'I see you have wasted no time, my Meg. Were there any problems?'

'None. I left a message for The Lady Elizabeth that I had received news of an aunt in the country who had fallen sick and required my help. I thought it best not to just walk out. My disappearance could have looked like flight.'

'That's true. The Princess will readily accept the excuse and will not raise a hue and cry if you are found to be missing. I need time to move before there is any likelihood of pursuit.'

She was startled, he saw and he decided to give her a brief explanation of his conduct.

'I was once in the service of the Duke of Clarence, the King's brother.' Her eyes widened but she made no comment. 'Since his death I have been anxious about his children, The Lady Margaret and the young Earl of Warwick. Indeed it was for this reason that I first came to England. I needed to assure myself of their safety.'

'You were afraid the King would harm them?'

'I feared it. For reasons which I cannot disclose to you now, the children are an embarrassment both to him and to the Queen and all members of her family. I asked you to trust me. When I have Gloucester's permission to speak, I will explain more fully. My fears were groundless. The King kept the children safe, but now he is dead they are no longer under his protection. There remain others who would wish them underground.'

'Oh no—'

'We must not be squeamish, Meg. Children are dangerous if they stand in the way of men's ambitions.'

'But Gloucester—'

'I have no fears for them in his hands but he is not here and will not be for some days. The children are lodged at the Tower again since their guardian at present is the Marquess of Dorset, the Queen's son.'

'And you do not trust him?'

'No.'

'You will rescue the children? But—'

'It will be hazardous. Your part will be to convey them to Sir Piers Langham in Kent. They need the care of a woman. Will you risk this for me?'

'You need not to ask—' She broke off as they heard the sound of iron carriage wheels

116

and Beaumont went to the window.

'Gaveston has provided my carriage. Don your cloak, Meg. Bess has a basket of food for the journey. I hope to have the children safely out of London by nightfall. I will accompany you to the first inn and see you safe on your way tomorrow. Then I must circumnavigate London and ride to meet Gloucester.'

She nodded and, rising, obeyed him, lifting the bundle without question to follow him below. He took it from her and approved its lightness. Margaret Woollat was a practical woman. She was not fool enough to encumber him with useless fripperies.

An ill-assorted pair stood by the coach awaiting Beaumont's inspection. The man who came forward was short and squat. He bore the unmistakable marks of the hired soldier. He was warmly clad in leathern coat and high thigh boots. His hood was pushed back to reveal his thinning hair of indeterminate colour. His walk was a curious roll. Beaumont smiled at the almost villainous cast of the features. One eye had been gouged out by a straying arrow and the man's attempt to focus his surviving one gave the impression of low cunning, probably unjustified. Beaumont felt Margaret give a little gasp behind him as she averted her face from the scar which ran raggedly from the man's ruined eye-socket to the left side of his mouth. The newcomer smiled, somewhat twistedly, due to the puckering made by the scar, but the smile was genuine enough. He pulled his forelock respectfully and addressed himself to Beaumont in a voice unusually soft for one of his appearance.

'Sir John Gaveston presents his compliments, sir. I was a bowman in his company at Barnet. I'm to go where you wish and serve you to the best of my ability and without question. I'm Simon Oates, begging your lordship's pardon.' He turned and indicated his companion, a tall, bent, elderly man who remained by the horses. 'Roger Wilkins, sir, our coachman. He could drive you through 'ell itself.'

'I trust he won't be needed to,' Beaumont said caustically. He nodded to the man and moved to assist Margaret into the coach. Oates sprang to attention immediately and offered his arm. She hesitated for a moment then looked directly at the grey eye, caught the unmistakable twinkle of humour, and smiled in answer. She seated herself and bestowed her bundle by her feet. Bess came bustling from the inn with a covered basket of provisions.

'Father says, are you to return here, sir, before you ride to Northampton?'

Beaumont handed the basket to Margaret. 'Tell him I think that unlikely, Bess. I'm in haste to meet His Grace of Gloucester. I'll leave my belongings here and pay my reckoning when next I'm in London. Will he

118

trust me that far?'

'Surely, Sir Charles. God speed.'

Wilkins climbed ponderously to the driving seat and Oates mounted his grey, a horse as uncertain of colour as the man himself. Beaumont noted the fact grimly. It would stand them in good stead in the future if they were pursued. Oates and his steed would hardly be noticed and would fade into the background of any witness's mind the moment they had passed from his sight. He mounted his own horse, dismissing the groom who'd held him. In the gloom of the coach interior he was reassured to see Margaret's expression was grave but confident.

At the Tower he dismounted and with Oates in attendance went in search of the guard captain. He was fortunate to be greeted by Gaveston.

'I come on business of my Lord of Dorset,' Beaumont said hoarsely, his face shadowed by his round-brimmed hat.

'I have instructions concerning you.' Gaveston's tone was brisk. 'Here is your authority.' He handed Beaumont a roll of parchment from which descended several official seals. 'Come this way. The children are lodged in the lieutenant's house. It was warmer there.'

They crossed the grassy courtyard and waited while Gaveston knocked at the heavy iron door. A raven cawed disconsolately.

Again Beaumont shivered. He could not rid himself of his dislike of the huge black birds. They seemed omens of doom. The door swung open and Gaveston stepped into the lieutenant's house and waited for Beaumont and Oates to follow. A serving man conducted them to a chill room where the nurse Beaumont had met before sat with the children before a meagre fire, which gave little warmth even close to the massive fireplace.

Beaumont wasted no words. 'I've my Lord of Dorset's authority to take the children,' he said, holding out the sealed parchment.

The woman glanced at it and raised her eyes to the serving man, who now stood by the door. He was a thin, stooping individual, and his head poked forward as if constantly searching into the affairs of others. Beaumont cast him a backward glance and lowered his own blue eyes before the hooded gaze of the other man—a creature of Dorset's undoubtedly.

Oates gave a short bark of a laugh as the woman regarded the messenger with pursed lips, uncertain how to proceed.

'Come, mother, what are you waiting for? We had our orders as you had yours.' He rolled his one eye to the children who had withdrawn slightly behind their guardian. The Lady Margaret jerked her head nervously at sight of him and the sound of his strange hissing cadences. She put out a hand to clutch at the

120

nurse's skirts. The young Earl stood still, unmoving, his eyes on the two visitors.

'You're early,' the woman said at last, 'I've not completed the packing. I wasn't expecting you until the morning.'

Beaumont shrugged, a gesture insolent and betraying impatience. 'Haste is preferable. As for baggage, they will need little.'

The woman peered across the room at him sharply. He could feel her attempting to gauge his expression, deliberately hidden from her by the concealing liripipe of his hat. Was it a fleeting sign of regret he noted or was she merely suspicious and anxious to be convinced of his authority?

The serving man spoke from the doorway. 'Get their cloaks, Gertrude. The Marquess stressed there were to be no questions.' His eyes flickered ferret-like over Oates's sturdy form and registered approval at his Lord's choice of servant.

The woman rose and went into a smaller chamber. She brushed off the girl's frantically clinging fingers and the child came forward a little, shielding her brother with her young body.

'Where do you take us, sir?' she said. There was a suggestion of a tremor in the clear, high voice, but she was resolute and there was no trace of tears.

'To a safe place, Highness,' Beaumont said shortly. 'London is in a state of unrest. Your

121

uncle requires you to be out of the city.'

'My uncle the King is dead?'

'Yes.'

She flinched at his bluntness. 'But my other uncle Gloucester will take care of us.'

'Likely so, lady. For the present I have my orders.'

The nurse came back with travelling cloaks. The children stood docilely while she put them on. She gave the princess a little push as the child stood, hesitant. Beaumont reached out and clasped her small, cold fingers.

'Take the boy,' he ordered Oates and turned to the door. Behind him he heard young Warwick give a strangled cry as Oates picked him up unceremoniously. The serving man still stood with his back to the door watching them both covertly.

'You were paid?' he said at last.

'Aye, generously.'

'Then see that you make no mistakes.' He stood back as the two passed through with the children. Gaveston waited near the outer door. He glanced briefly at the cloaked young figures, nodded once to Beaumont then stood aside as the little group moved unhurriedly to the waiting coach.

Wilkins stood by the open coach door. Beaumont lifted up the Lady Margaret and turned as Oates came up behind him with the young Earl. He barked a swift command to Meg. 'Don't talk to them about anything. Try

122

to keep them quiet.'

Wilkins went to the driving box, threw a coin at a boy who'd been holding his horses, then prepared to drive off.

'Eltham,' Beaumont said quietly. 'Take it easy. We must appear to be in no haste. We'll choose a quiet inn, but not one which will note every visitor as a rarity. Let us go.'

The light had almost faded now. If they wished to leave the city before total darkness they must make some speed. Already the streets were emptying so their way was not hindered by farm carts now empty of produce. Once out on the open road Wilkins whipped up his horses and made a steady speed. Beaumont rode by the wide of the swaying carriage. He was concerned in case Meg was having to deal with hysterics, but she allowed herself to be seen briefly, pushing back the leathern curtains which closed off the interior from the view of passers-by. The young Earl was frightened, that was plain and the little princess by no means reassured, but both had been brought up in a hard school. They would obey without question and for this factor he was grateful. It increased their chances of success. To have talked with the children outside the Tower, where he might have been overheard, would have been foolhardy in the extreme. He must trust to the remembrance of his other visit, almost four years ago as he explained to the Lady Margaret when they arrived at the inn

123

where he would choose to spend the night.

'The Green Man' at Eltham seemed a suitable hostelry. It was neither crowded nor completely lacking in guests. Their host would have enough to occupy his mind, beside the little party of soberly dressed folk who desired to spend one night. Beaumont bespoke a private chamber. Wilkins tacitly agreed to stay with the horses. Oates took the bridles of his own and Charles's mounts. He nodded when Beaumont ordered him to present himself inside when he could. He drew the young Earl inside but felt the chilled fingers pulling against his own. The Lady Margaret came quietly enough with Meg. He had ordered food to be brought to their room and went straight up the narrow stair after a slatternly chamber-maid.

Meg gave an exclamation of irritation as she loosed the princess's hand and went to the bed. The sheets were reasonably clean, though damp. They must be aired before the children could sleep there. She challenged the sulky looking wench and sent her running down the stair for sea-coal for the fireplace. The young Earl backed from them until he came up short against the far wall. He was still slow and his movements puppet-like, but there was understanding in the grey-blue eyes. The boy, thank God, was not an idiot, as Beaumont might have feared, but would be dull of wits, one who would need patience in handling. He *would* learn, but he was not of the stuff of

124

Kings. Beaumont's conscience smote him as he saw the boy's eyes stare at him with a kind of dawning horror. He decided to address himself to the princess.

'My lady, have no fear for you or your brother. I am Sir Charles Beaumont and once served your father. You will remember I visited you once some years ago.' He had put aside his concealing hat and thrown back his cloak.

She regarded him with a frown of concentration, oddly adult for one scarcely ten years of age. Her gaze was somewhat myopic but challenging and direct. At the end he felt he had her trust, but rather she gave it since there was naught else she could do, than that she did so willingly.

'I think I do, sir. You brought me a doll.'

He smiled. 'From Burgundy. You remember. That is well.'

'Again I ask where you are taking us, sir?'

'To a friend of mine who lives in Kent. He has children of his own. His wife will love you. Later they will bring you to London into the care of your uncle, Gloucester.'

She was silent for a spell, then she apparently accepted his plan for she went to her brother who had edged away from Meg, who was attempting to divest him of his cloak.

The older child bent down an whispered something in his ear. He lifted his head and looked steadily at Beaumont. Sir Charles flushed and moved uneasily under the boy's scrutiny. God willing he would keep faith with these two, if it cost him his head.

A knock at the stout door told him that food he had ordered had arrived and he called a peremptory, 'Come in,' and turned to divest himself of his own cloak. He kept his sword buckled in position. Meg had taken charge of the domestic arrangements. She gave him a tight-lipped smile of understanding and waspishly ordered the inn-wench to air the sheets and keep the newly lit fire bright.

They all ate without much talk. Half-way through the meal, Oates knocked and Beaumont left Meg with her charges and went to talk with him outside.

'He's arrived, Dorset's man.'

'In the tap-room?'

The soldier nodded and lowered his voice. 'He rode in about a quarter of an hour ago. He went to the stables first, I reckon, to identify our horses. Since he did not come to the Tower Gate-house, he must have had other spies on duty there.'

Beaumont considered. 'Go down and drink with him. I'll join you later. Greet him as an old friend. We're no fools. We expected our master to check on us. He'll swallow our talk.'

The man nodded and clattered down the stair. Beaumont went back to Meg.

'Get to bed, sweeting,' he said quietly. 'The children will sleep sound with you. I'll be up shortly.'

She came to the door anxiously. The Princess looked up from her task of peeling a wizened apple for her brother. She had accepted her position as protectress, and mentor. She was worried but made no move to come to them.

Beaumont was relieved that she was disinclined to panic. He told Meg the truth.

'We were followed.'

Alarm leaped to her eyes and he smiled, though that smile did not reach his eyes.

'Do not concern yourself. All will be well. Later I'll come up and sleep in the chair beside you. Until then I'll send Oates to wait outside the door.'

In the tap-room doorway he paused and looked round for his quarry. In obedience to his orders, Oates was sitting with the man in a corner behind the door. Beaumont walked over and stood silently regarding him, his eyes half-closed. The other's gaze flickered over him not without some embarrassment.

'So,' Beaumont said deliberately, 'we are not trusted?'

'Nay, I'll not say that.'

Beaumont grinned mirthlessly and signalled for the inn-wench to come close. 'Then what is your reason for being here, friend?'

Dorset's creature blinked nervously and again Beaumont laughed without humour. 'Get upstairs,' he said to Oates. 'Guard the door. I want no one to see our charges or talk

127

with them.'

Oates stood up unwillingly. His one eye betrayed his concern but Beaumont shrugged impatiently and he went off, walking with that sailorly roll, so familiar to the man.

The wench came with jacks of ale, but Beaumont shook his head. 'Nay, lass, we'll have mulled wine to keep out the cold.'

She shook back her hair in irritation at the need for a second journey and stamped off to the kitchen. Beaumont leaned back on his chair and surveyed his companion smilingly.

'Come, my friend, you are nervous. There's no need. The job shall be done and you will ride back with the news tomorrow.'

'As soon as that?' The man muttered the question and traced a finger in spilled ale on the rough table-top, avoiding Beaumont's eyes.

'The sooner the news reaches—our dear master,' he paused before the words, 'the sooner my payment is complete.'

'Aye.'

'You find the suggestion distasteful?'

'The work is for butchers!'

'You betray a fatal weakness, man—pity.'

'Nay, the children stand in the way—'

'Aye.'

The man shuffled his feet as the wench banged down the wine jug and minced off to the kitchen once more. Beaumont poured wine and the other took the cup with a hand which shook slightly.

'You plan to do the job—here?'

Beaumont drank deep before replying. 'You will spill wine. That is stupid waste.'

'Where—the inn is crowded?'

'You and I will leave in a moment and search for a suitable spot. There must be barns in plenty. Early in the morning—' He paused and shrugged again. 'If you stay and see the evidence, your master will be the more sure of us.'

The man took a strangled gulp of wine. 'That will not be necessary.'

'But wiser, my friend, wiser.' He watched as the other drank deep of the cup. He appeared to drink rather than engage himself in conversation he found disturbing to his peace. However, he waved away Beaumont's hand when he offered to refill the cup.

'You are sure? Well, then, let us go.' Beaumont rose and placed a firm hand on the man's elbow. He smiled as the man prepared to expostulate, then he gave way, rose and accompanied Beaumont from the inn. 'We shall not be long. It would be impossible to walk far with our victims.' He affected to ignore the other's wince at his outspokenness. 'There are barns over there on the opposite side of the road. One might serve our purpose.'

'Too close to the inn. The innkeeper—'

'Will keep his mouth closed for the same reason that both of us will keep ours. If necessary I'll ensure his silence.'

129

The man turned in the moonlight. 'My master chose you well.'

Beaumont's lips curved in that travesty of a smile, the other found so disconcerting. 'I was well recommended,' he said gently.

The road was clear and the ditch was not difficult to jump. The meadow on the far side sloped down from the path. The grass was wet with the mist of evening and the two kept behind the hedge while they headed for the outbuildings they saw loom in the distance.

The first was barred and chained. Beaumont shook his head as he tested the staple then beckoned his companion on.

'Why is it necessary—?'

'The ground is too hard. There'll be a frost again tonight. I must dispose of the evidence. The ground will be softer within.'

The man's face loomed up at him in the moon-glow. His head was thrust forward in the characteristic pose Beaumont remembered from seeing him that first time in the lieutenant's lodging.

'If this should be discovered too soon—'

'Tush, man, there are three of us to complete the work. You'll be able to carry the news that the children sleep well.'

He eased back the wooden bar across the door of the other barn and pushed open the door. It creaked partly wide then stuck fast. The ground beneath had risen with the damp and frost. He stood back and gestured the spy

130

to precede him.

'Let us examine the ground. It seems our farmer has used this to store grain. There is little left. Fortunate for us. We can find a spot where the soil is unlikely to be disturbed, behind the door, possibly.'

The man stood uncertainly in the doorway, peering towards the dark corner Beaumont indicated.

'Try the ground, man. If it's soft enough, it will suit our purpose. Did you note the position of the barn? Later you will be able to recall it. Such information might be useful for you.'

The man turned his head sharply at the satirical note in Beaumont's voice, but he could make nothing of his expression. His face was in shadow.

'Such information might guard me against *you* too,' he said coldly.

He saw the other's shoulders rise and fall, a black silhouette against the uncertain light of the half-opened door. Irritated by the hired killer's mockery, he gave his attention to the condition of the ground. He would be more comfortable at the inn, and more so early tomorrow when his task of supervision was done and he could ride back to London with his tidings. The man's barbed thrusts disturbed him more than he could explain.

He half stumbled over the handle of some implement which had fallen behind the door, cursed roundly and attempted to rise from his sprawled position.

Beaumont came up behind him and he threw up one hand to demand silently his assistance. He had no warning of the hand that killed him almost instantly, without a cry. There was a cold, sharp pain between his shoulder blades, a choke, a bubble of bloody froth to the lips then he knew nothing more.

Beaumont withdrew his dagger blade and cleaned it without haste on the man's cloak. He felt no regret. He stirred the sprawled body with the toe of one boot, stood looking down for a moment, then he walked steadily to the bar door and outside. The door resisted his efforts to push it close for some time but he placed his shoulder against it and shoved hard. At last it gave and he re-barred it. It might be days before the store barn was used again, but if not, it would be no matter. By first light Meg would be on her way. It was hardly likely the man would be missed.

The innkeeper was harassed when Beaumont sleepily declared some minutes later that he'd go to bed.

'You've been out, sir?'

'To the stables. My driver does not always keep to my instructions.' He looked round. 'I see my drinking companion has left.'

'Your pardon, sir?'

'The man who drank wine with me.'

'I confess, sir, I did not note him. We have been busy tonight.'

132

'No matter, just a passing meeting. I thought he intended to lodge here.'

'I fear not, sir. We have no room.'

Beaumont smiled genially. 'A pity, we could have ridden together. No doubt he has sought other accommodation. Good night, innkeeper.'

'Sleep well, sir.'

The man bowed as he handed a rush-light holder to his guest and Beaumont mounted the stairs. Oates stirred from his position near the door.

'All is well. He's gone to his master.' Beaumont stooped to whisper in the archer's ear. The man grinned up at the wry twist of the lips, revealed to him by the rush-light's flicker.

'Earlier than expected.'

'Aye, by some years or months, who could tell? Have you a blanket? Can you stay here?'

'I've my cloak, sir. I'll be comfortable enough. There's been no sound from inside.'

Beaumont nodded. 'I stopped to look in the stables. Wilkins is snug enough. We leave at cock-crow. I shall escort you some five miles, then leave for Northampton.'

'Your charges will be safe with us.'

'Mistress Woollat will have full instructions. You are to let nothing delay you until all are safe with Sir Piers Langham.'

'I know that, sir.'

Beaumont gripped his shoulder in a light clasp then as quietly as possible let himself into

133

the chamber.

Meg had left the rush-light burning, but it had burnt low. He held up his fresh one and smiled down at her. The children lay on the inside of the bed. Meg moved and half sat up.

He put a finger on his lip and shook his head at the question in her eyes. In the uncertain light he saw her brows draw together as if in doubt. She had not missed the hard glitter in those eyes she knew so well. Her gaze travelled downwards to the dagger in his belt. His smile did not fade.

The little princess stirred sleepily and gently Meg replaced the bed covering round her shoulders, reassuring her with a gentle pressure of her hand. Suddenly her eyes widened and he knew she understood.

He settled himself in the chair by the bed and extinguished the rush-light.

CHAPTER ELEVEN

Jake Garnet was puzzled but pleased to greet Beaumont when he rode into the courtyard of 'The Golden Cockerel' four days after he had left it.

Beaumont gave Phoebus into the charge of the ostler and accompanied him into the tap-room.

'I changed my mind and decided to return to

London for some days. I have heard that The Duke of Gloucester will stay possibly in York to celebrate a requiem for the soul of the late King. It would be pointless for me to kick my heels in Northampton for days. I shall be more usefully employed in viewing the situation here in the capital.'

Garnet nodded and went with him to the chamber where he'd left his baggage, calling to Bess in the kitchen as he did so to prepare dinner for Sir Charles.

'All is as you left it, sir. No one has lodged in your room. Have things gone well?'

'Very well, Jake. Mistress Woollat will soon be with Sir Piers and Lady Langham. While she is under their protection I have no fears for her. I escorted her half the way, then left her to Oates and Wilkins. I have assured myself those two can be trusted.'

'You'll stay here then, with us till you ride north?'

'Certainly. I'll retire after dinner. I need a long sleep. In the morning I'll present myself to Lord Hastings at Westminster. That way I shall know what news of the court to report to his Grace. What talk is there in the city? Come, man, give me all the news while I rest.'

Garnet pursed his lips thoughtfully as Beaumont stretched himself on the bed, after kicking off his riding boots.

'We hear all sorts of rumours. 'Tis said My Lord the Marquess of Dorset has removed

135

treasure and money from the Tower.'

'Man, that would be treason without consent of the Regent or at least the concurrence of the full council in session.'

'Like as not, it's just talk, sir. He's equipped men enough for a private army. That I know to be true.' The innkeeper's face was grave. 'He's Constable of the Tower, don't forget, and the young King's brother. He's declared his actions are in defence of the realm against any attack from the French.'

Beaumont grimaced. 'He takes much upon himself. I pray His Grace of Gloucester looks to the defence of his own person. This raising of a private force smacks of a desire to take charge of The King's Grace when he enters London.'

'Aye.' Garnet sighed. He could still recollect the troublous times when lord fought against lord. He descended the stairs heavily. He could see the same pattern repeating itself. It was a bad day for England when the King died leaving his heir yet so young.

After dinner Beaumont barred his chamber door and prepared for sleep. He'd had little or none since the day he'd entered London and heard of the death of the King. While Meg and the children had been in his charge, he had not allowed himself to do more than rest his eyes. Now sleep evaded him.

He told himself Meg was safe enough. Soon he would hold her in his arms again. Only once during those last days had he dared to do so. After breakfast at 'The Green Man' he had sent the two children down to the coach with Oates. The young Earl appeared to have a great love of horses, though Beaumont was amazed to discover from his talk that he could not yet ride. His education had been grossly neglected. Oates promised him a visit to the stables and the children went willingly enough.

Beaumont turned to Meg, now cloaked and ready for the journey. She came to his arms like a homing bird, and he thrust back her hood, glad that she wore no elaborate hennin today and he could loosen the folds of her wimple and touch her thick, brown hair.

'Not long now, my Meg,' he said hoarsely.

'The man—last night, you killed him?'

'I had to. He was a creature of Dorset's. He openly admitted that he came here to make sure we murdered the children.'

Her face blanched as she peered up into his face. 'He thought you—'

'Aye, lass. Why else do you think we were entrusted with them?'

'But—Charles, they aren't safe even now—'

'Royal children are seldom safe, my heart. With Sir Piers they are as safe as they are ever likely to be.'

'You wish me to stay with them?'

He shook his head. 'No. Gloucester will soon arrive in London. It is unlikely he will retire to Middleham now for some time.

Doubtless The Duchess will join him, probably at Crosby Place. The Duke bought the property recently. Indeed I was commissioned on this errand to visit the house and report on its readiness for habitation. Either Sir Piers will join the Duke in London and you can return with him, or, if not, he will provide an escort for you.' He grinned. 'Despite his unprepossessing countenance I would trust Oates to Hell and back. If you cannot come to me I swear I will fetch you.'

She lifted her hand and traced the outlines of his lips and chin with her fingers. 'For what purpose, Charles?'

He bent his head and kissed her lips, then, his passion rising, her throat and lower, where her snowy breast was revealed by the fashionably low cut of her gown. 'You will be mine, Meg, as you wish, though God knows you are too good for such a life.'

'Be good to me for but a few years, my love, and I will be content.' Her voice was clear without a falter.

He gave her letters and instructions to give Sir Piers and then they had descended the stair to the inn parlour. Though he had escorted her further, they had no more opportunity to speak privately.

Meg would be his. Gloucester had been generous over these last years. She would want for nothing. He would find her a small house. Jake Garnet would know of such a one.

Thinking so he fell asleep at last.

Though his dark blue velvet doublet could not be considered garish by any stretch of the imagination, he felt conspicuous as he walked the quietened corridors of the Palace of Westminster the following day. All members of the court he encountered were clad in deepest mourning and the usual high buzz of laughter was stilled. Even now it seemed impossible that that golden giant of a King was no more.

A page escorted him to the Lord Chamberlain's apartments and soberly requested that he wait in a small ante-room. Beaumont sat, prepared to wait some time. Undoubtedly, My Lord Hastings would have much of the King's business to occupy his mind.

He was surprised when the Lord Chamberlain came to the inner door and gestured him to enter. Hastings was dressed in slovenly fashion, possibly in haste as the hour was relatively early. Beaumont remembered him from the old days, the gay jesting companion to the King. Now there were lines of dissipation and anxiety round the deep-set eyes and touches of grey at the temple and above the ears mingling with the brown elegantly waved hair.

'Beaumont, come in, man. You ride from Middleham?'

'I do, My Lord. I carry letters from His

Grace of Gloucester to the King.'

'You have heard, of course?'

'Yes, My Lord, though I have only just entered London I came to you at once, since the news may be of some urgency and need to be placed before council.'

Hastings nodded, handled the sealed letter with some hesitancy, then excused himself, broke the seals and lowered his head to read. Beaumont noted the fine appointments of the room. The King had done well by his favourite. Hastings had prospered. It was no wonder that genuine sorrow was written across the handsome dissolute face. He had fought with the King, bled with him, wenched with him. He would miss his glorious sovereign deeply. His black velvet doublet was cut in the height of fashion, the sleeves slashed with white silk and embroidered with silver thread. The collar was undone and the whole attire showed a lack of attention. True the tailor must have been summoned in haste to cut such a mourning garment, but it was as fashionable as ever. Hastings had had little sleep last night or had sat up late and lingered abed this morning. It was not like him to receive a visitor without checking his appearance for the slightest fault.

He sighed and laid down the letter. 'This contains nothing of urgency, private messages of love, assurances of loyalty and a report on the border situation. I hear you have had a tour of duty at Berwick.'

'Yes, My Lord. All is quiet at present. That part of the realm need not disturb you.'

'Praise be to God,' Hastings muttered. 'That at least is certain.'

'Have you work for me, My Lord?'

'Do you ride back to greet his Grace?'

'I had thought to ride to Northampton. I hear The Duke will take charge of the young King there.'

Hastings jerked up his chin abruptly. 'That is his intention,' he said. His tone had an inflection Beaumont did not like but he moved no muscle of his countenance and waited for further instructions.

'Ride to Northampton. Warn the Duke of possible dissension in the city.'

'My Lord?'

'There is no time for soft words. The Queen and Dorset have already issued patents to collect taxes. No mention of His Grace of Gloucester was made, neither was he mentioned in the bidding prayer written for the convention of Bishops. The Queen considers herself Regent, guided and ruled by Dorset, and the coronation of the King is fixed for May 4th.'

'Early, My Lord. Can arrangements—'

'Too early, Sir Charles. I have read the King's will in Council. His Grace of Gloucester was there named as Lord Protector of England, and ill it will be for England if he fails to fulfil this role.'

141

'You expected these happenings, sir?'

'I had no expectation of the King's sudden death. Had I any warnings of serious illness, I would have summoned His Grace of Gloucester south before now.'

Beaumont rose and bowed. 'I understand, My Lord. I will acquaint his Grace with your news as soon as possible.'

'Aye man, go speedily. Since I must change masters, I'll serve a Plantagenet.'

At the door Beaumont turned. ' 'Tis hoped the Queen and Royal children are well, in spite of their natural sorrow.'

'The Queen is well, sir.'

'And her royal charges, the Duke of Clarence's children? The Duke of Gloucester will hold himself responsible now for the safe keeping of his brother's children—all of them.'

Hastings looked puzzled. 'True enough. The Marquess of Dorset has charge of them. They are lodged in the Tower, I understand.'

Beaumont's blue eyes held those of the Lord Chamberlain for some moments, then he bowed again and withdrew.

Almost at once he realised his mistake. He had left by a door opposite from the one which he had entered. He found himself now in a further beautifully furnished room. The floors carpeted, the tapestries bright with jewel-like colours. A woman was seated by the fireplace. She looked up at him, a smile curving her lips, hastily subdued as she failed to recognise the man she expected.

Seldom at a loss, Beaumont bowed courteously. She answered with a queenly inclination of the head. Like all those at court she was clad in deepest mourning, the white folds of her wimple contrasting simply. She was very lovely. Even seated as she was, he realised that she carried herself regally, despite her undoubted lack of breeding. Her mouth was demurely held in a solemn line, though he thought it could at any moment break into laughter. Jane Shore, the goldsmith's wife, the King's merry mistress, must not betray amusement at such a time. She watched him out of the farther door without moving.

He left Westminster in thoughtful mood. So Meg had not been mistaken. Hastings had shared more than gold with his royal master. Had the King known of his Chamberlain's association with the noted beauty? The question was, had Meg been right when she'd coupled Jane Shore's name with Dorset? If so, where did the lovely woman's allegiance lie now—with Hastings or the Woodvilles? It was too soon in the game to be certain.

CHAPTER TWELVE

Beaumont was filthy and tired when he drew rein in York, at The Earl of Warwick's town house. He stumbled stiff from the saddle as the groom took his horse in charge. Despite his bone-weariness, his heart pounded with thankfulness. He had ridden almost without rest once he had realised the urgency of Hastings' need to have Gloucester in London well primed beforehand of the situation he must face. It seemed impossible that he might yet be in time, but the news that the Duke was yet in York had spurred him on and now he paused in the doorway to catch his breath before announcing himself and his errand.

He was recognised and conveyed to a small chamber where he might wash. There Sir Francis Lovell came hurriedly to greet him.

'His Grace of Gloucester is yet at the Minster. He has spent long hours praying privately for the repose of the late King's soul. Charles, man, I thought you were in London.'

'It is imperative I see his Grace.'

'He is tired. The news has near broken his heart. Today we held a solemn requiem. Yesterday he summoned all nobles in the region to declare their allegiance to the young King. He intends to leave at first light. Can he not rest this evening? Will not your report wait?'

'No, Sir Francis, it cannot. Tomorrow it may be difficult to speak with his Grace privately. The ride may bring a press of nobles round him. Later—'

Lovell nodded. 'I'll announce you when he

returns. I've ordered food. Eat well and rest. I'll try to find you a lodging in the town. Truth to say it will not be easy. Every inn is packed to the roof.'

Beaumont smiled faintly. 'I'll sleep in the stables if need be.'

'Aye.' Lovell made as if to say more than clucked his teeth impatiently and went out of the room.

Beaumont was ravenous. He had not eaten all day. He'd gone without breakfast save a jack of ale in order to be in the saddle by cock-crow. He set to when the page brought cold meats, pies, and sweet malmsey. He did not turn when the door opened behind him but said through a mouthful of venison pasty, 'If it's fruit, put it on the table, lad.'

'I think that will come later, Charles.'

Beaumont swung round to stare at Gloucester who had quietly entered. He was pale but composed, a stately sombre figure in unrelieved mourning. He came to the seat opposite Charles and seated himself, waving Beaumont to continue to remain seated.

'Sit and eat, Charles. I hear you are sharp-set and exhausted. I can wait for your news.'

'Nay, sir. I begged Sir Francis the privilege of seeing you before you retire.'

'You bring letters from Hastings? He has informed me that the young King should reach Northampton by the twenty-sixth or twenty-seventh of the month. He will await me there.

145

Are there delays?'

'Not that I know of, your Grace. My Lord Rivers was to bring the King as the Council dictated. His desire to take an army was refused. Even so he brings two thousand men and a train of artillery.'

'So.' Gloucester's eyebrows met expressively but he said nothing.

'The townsfolk murmur. They fear another minority.'

'That is natural enough. It cannot be avoided unfortunately.'

'The Queen and Dorset are acting as Regents in your absence. The King's will has been virtually thrust aside. The army and navy have been strengthened by funds taken by Dorset from the Tower treasury. My Lord Hastings bids you ride to London well armed.'

'I have a sizeable escort.'

'Nothing like two thousand men-at-arms?'

'No—about six hundred, I would say. It seemed unnecessary to demand more since our combined forces will guard the King.'

'And if Earl Rivers wishes to keep control of the King, sir? What then?'

Beaumont felt Gloucester stiffen though he made no move to rise. One hand fingered his ring, a gesture Beaumont had noted as usual with him in moments of stress.

'The King's will was quite clear, Sir Charles. Lord Hastings sent me a fair copy. The King's Grace named me as Lord Protector of the

Realm and guardian of his children.'

'Aye, sir, in the teeth of his wife's objections to such an act.'

Gloucester's voice remained calm. 'It is understandable the Queen should feel so. We were never close.'

'You were well warned, sir. I have delivered to you Lord Hastings' forebodings.'

'And you have done well, Sir Charles. I am truly grateful. You must be tired. I suggest you sleep in my apartments. A bed can be put up for you.'

'My Lord, that will not be necessary. Sir Francis Lovell has promised to send out a servant to enquire in the town.'

Gloucester waved away his protest. 'It would be a fruitless search. The town is filled with Yorkshire gentles. I have called them to swear their allegiance to the new King. I insist.' He smiled bleakly. 'Since you are so hot in my defence, I could have no finer watchdog. Will you ride with us tomorrow? If you are too wearied—'

'No, sir. I wish to accompany you.'

Gloucester rose and Charles hastily sprang up, as etiquette demanded. 'Then I will leave you.'

'Sir, one moment. I asked Sir Francis for this interview since I wished to speak on another matter—privately.'

'Well, sir?'

'Are we truly alone? None could eavesdrop?'

Gloucester's eyebrows rose in interrogation. He walked to the door, and flinging it open, dismissed a man-at-arms on guard, then re-closed the door and barred it.

'None will intrude on us now. Speak.'

'You will consider it strange that I did not ride immediately for Middleham with news of the King's death. The truth is, sir, I had business which could not wait even on that.'

A gleam appeared in Gloucester's grey-green eyes. He seated himself and gestured for Beaumont to do likewise.

'The Clarence children are safe?'

'They are now, sir, with Sir Piers Langham. He has orders to keep charge of them until you personally order him to surrender them.'

'So, you considered their danger acute?'

'I was not in error, sir. Their lives were threatened. I have evidence. That I will place before you in due time.' He took a breath before continuing. 'It is the reason *why* they were in danger which concerns us.'

Gloucester's lips parted slightly. His eyes did not leave Beaumont's face. One hand tensed, then the fingers relaxed on the table-top.

Beaumont's sudden question took him unawares.

'Know you aught of Lady Eleanor Butler, sir?'

Puzzled by the change of subject the Duke's eyes opened wide in surprise. 'She was daughter of The Earl of Shrewsbury, a beauty,

148

I understand, widowed, her husband being Sir Thomas Butler. What of her?'

'As you said, sir, a noted beauty.'

Gloucester frowned. He stared across at Beaumont's intent expression then shrugged. 'Another paramour of my brother the King? Highly possible, Sir Charles. I knew nothing of the matter. I was over-young at the time. Do you tell me there is yet another Royal bastard to consider?'

Beaumont shook his head gently. 'No, sir. The lady entered a nunnery. There were no children to my knowledge. She died in 1466.'

'Then if there are no problems—?'

'My Lord, the King was contracted to her in marriage. There were witnesses. The Duke of Clarence knew this and your Lady Mother.'

The Duke made no answer. Beaumont looked uneasily across the table at the pale, controlled countenance opposite. The eyes were wide, the mouth held in tightly as if to keep in any protest the owner might make at the pain the blow had dealt him. At last the stare lessened. He put up one hand to his forehead.

'The marriage to Elizabeth Grey. He *knew* it was no marriage? You tell me my own brother *knew* he was committing bigamy—that his children—God in Heaven, I'll not accept it. You repeat some libellous fishwife gossip—'

'Gossip it may be, My Lord, but from no fishwife. I was body squire to His Grace of

149

Clarence, near to him both night and day. What he told me in confidence I did not divulge.'

Gloucester rose and walked awkwardly to the window. It was the first time since his return to England that Beaumont was made aware of that old childish accident which had twisted one leg, so that the Duke halted somewhat in his gait. It had improved so much of late that he had thought him cured. He had danced at Middleham, partnered his own wife and The Lady Elizabeth. The limp had not then been noticeable. Now the sudden stress of emotion, or tiredness after the long hours of duty and prayer in the Minster, had cramped the limb and for the moment Gloucester seemed the crook-backed cripple his enemies were wont to contemptuously label him. Beaumont appealed to his reason, that logical practicality which made him one of the shrewdest generals in the realm.

'Why, think you, did Clarence die so in the Tower?'

'You ask me now to believe that my brother had him murdered. Is that it?' Gloucester's voice was oddly muffled.

'Not necessarily. Others knew the secret. Men died and violently because they knew. Why do you think the Queen is now so anxious to have her son crowned and anointed? The coronation is set before due preparation can be made, before the boy has hardly time to enter

150

his own capital. Anointed he will be less easily set aside.'

Gloucester half turned. 'That is true, the sooner the better.

'You would have him crowned—a bastard?' Beaumont's cry was from the heart.

'Guard your tongue, Beaumont.' Gloucester's face was in shadow but his voice icy. 'Nay, man, I do not blame you for telling me this. I see your fears. They are very real. If Edward's children are—as you say—' Beaumont felt him almost wince at the suggestion, 'then young Warwick is—'

'He cannot reign, sir. You know that well enough.'

'Indeed he cannot. That is why you must keep silent. I do not even admit the truth of your story. I cannot without further consideration of the evidence, but were it so in fact, we have no alternative but to crown young Ned King. The Woodvilles, for once, are in the right of it. No useful purpose can be served by making such a tale public property. Warwick lies under attainder, and even if that were reversed I doubt his ability when grown to manhood to govern this realm wisely. It must be as I say.' He came forward and now Beaumont could see the grim determination on his face. His whole body trembled with suppressed anger, whether for his brother, whose foolishness had brought them to this pass, or against Beaumont, who had revealed the petty and shameful intrigue, he knew not.

'Answer me,' he snapped. 'You will obey me and repeat this to no man.'

Beaumont hesitated. He was uncertain how to broach what was in his heart. He lowered his eyes before the anger which sparked in the grey ones. 'I am your man in all things, sir. I shall do as you command me.'

Gloucester gave a faint sigh. He reached out and gripped Beaumont's elbow. 'Thank you,' he said quietly. Already the half smile had reappeared, now that the immediate danger of revelation was over. 'Come, let us to bed.'

In the blackness of Gloucester's bed-chamber, Beaumont tossed and turned on the pallet bed which had been put up there for him, hurriedly on the Duke's orders. He was exhausted but could not sleep. Icy sweat drenched his body under the linen covers. Had he done ill to ride back and repeat this pitiful tale to the man he now trusted above all others? He remembered the night he had heard it. Clarence had leaned across him with drunken, owlish, confidence and hiccupped the threads of the story, into his malmsey. He'd heard it from some singing boy who'd been present at the solemn betrothal. He'd laughed aloud at his squire's shocked expression and drank back the rest of the wine in a gulp. 'Ned was ever a fool for a pretty face,' he said with a chuckle. 'God, but I can see why he didn't make his contract known with our Cousin

Warwick breathing down his neck, impatient to seek a bride for him in the courts of Europe. Poor Ned. The girl most probably wept and sobbed and regretted the loss of her chastity. Ned was too much for her, I'll warrant. Then he met the pale and lovely Elizabeth. Ah well, she was not one to sell her favours short. So he married her.' Beaumont recalled how Clarence had sat and laughed to himself, and at he, Charles, sitting there silent. It had not proved a laughing matter in the end.

In the morning, Clarence had ordered him sharply to forget what had been said. He *had* done so, until the day he'd learnt of his master's death and the manner of it. He had not spoken of it since, until tonight. His hand clenched into a hard fist. It was not without possibility, that he too would die for having possession of it. Gloucester had been no more pleased to hear it, than he had himself, those long years ago. Yet now it had to be told. Gloucester must guard himself. He must know from whom he stood in peril and why.

The Duke stirred in his bed and sat up. He called quietly. 'Charles, are you awake?'

'Aye, sir.'

'Come to me.'

Beaumont rose, donned a robe lent to him by Sir Francis Lovell, covered his nakedness and came to the side of the Duke's bed.

'I cannot believe it of Ned.' The voice was still hoarse with emotion. 'Yet while I say the words, I doubt my own honesty. Such a course of action was not unlike him. He had to have Elizabeth Grey, then, when he was hot for her. I wonder how long it was before she discovered she was no wife.' He paused, then said with a half laugh, 'Perhaps Ned was not such a fool after all for a woman's wiles. He knew well enough he could not go through a solemn contract of marriage with Bona of Savoy. God, what would have been the outcome? Louis would have declared war on the instant. Edward's marriage at Grafton successfully foiled Warwick's determination to ally England to France and near enough wrecked the Yorkist cause.'

Beaumont was quiet, thinking.

Gloucester shot at him suddenly, 'That day, in the Tower, you had come to see young Warwick because you knew he was truly England's heir.'

Beaumont shifted uncertainly on his feet. '*One* of England's heirs, sir,' he reminded the Duke quietly. 'Clarence's children, as you say, lie under attainder.'

'Which could be reversed.'

'Yes.'

'Oh, Charles,' Gloucester's tone was faintly mocking in the darkness. 'You will never change. Clarence made you a gift of land. It was unfortunate you lost it in your fall from grace. In serving his son, you might gain an earldom at least.'

Beaumont's answer was harsh with restrained anger. 'You forget, My Lord, I have already agreed. Warwick cannot wear the crown.'

'Well?'

'My Lord Hastings remarked, sir, that ill it will be for England should you not take your place soon in London as protector of the realm. It occurs to me that it will be disastrous if the young King rejects your advice as he reaches his majority. I am not prepared to accept the fact that he is truly England's King.'

Gloucester's hand reached out and fastened cruelly on to his wrist. 'It occurs to me that there might have been another reason for your acceptance of service at Middleham. At the time I thought you concerned to be with the little serving wench.'

'And now?'

'Now, I *know* you are an ambitious man, Sir Charles. But rest content. With young Ned on the throne, and I the power behind it, I still have the ability to further those ambitions of yours.'

'Believe me, when I swear I will do no harm to your cause, sir. I am not the only one who wishes England to lie quiet under the guidance of a strong ruler.'

'It *will* do so, Sir Charles. That I promise you. I have sworn so to God in the peace of his Minster. I intend to keep that vow.'

CHAPTER THIRTEEN

Beaumont was smiling as he rode into Northampton and the man-at-arms in attendance who drew alongside when he beckoned, looked at him curiously. Gloucester had sent him ahead ostensibly with cordial greetings to Earl Rivers who was escorting the young King and joyful good wishes to the boy himself. In fact, Beaumont well knew his mission. It was some time since Gloucester had seen the young Edward who had been kept secluded at Ludlow far from court. Beaumont's grin widened. No wonder that the late King had considered it essential that his elder boy, now maturing to manhood, should be kept from the malicious tongues and sniggers of court officials who knew his father too well. Gloucester needed to know how best to greet the lad and win his confidence. He, Beaumont, could assess the situation and ride back with the necessary information.

He had not failed to note the black scowl on Sir Francis Lovell's face. Lovell had served the Duke loyally from boyhood. It was natural enough that he should resent now any signs of undue favour which Gloucester showed to his other gentleman. Had not Beaumont slept within the Duke's private chamber that last night in York? And several times during the ride south Gloucester had called Sir Charles to him and the two had conferred together. Sir Richard Ratcliffe had taken the matter more philosophically. Gloucester was fair and honourable with those who served him. Ratcliffe was content to await events.

There was little sign of activity in the town. Beaumont was puzzled. If the young King was in residence here he would have expected to see more people in the streets in the hopes of catching a glimpse of the youthful sovereign. The man-at-arms grunted when he passed a remark that the quietness was odd.

'Aye, sir. I'd thought to see the town crowded with folk pushing and farm carts blocking the way.'

'Ask at which inn the Royal party is lodged, Walter. I'll water the horses at this trough.'

The man dismounted and strode off towards the open doorway of a baker's shop, where the owner stood on the doorstep, his shirt sleeves, pushed well clear of floury elbows to talk with a neighbour.

Beaumont also dismounted and led the two animals to the water. He stooped and refreshed his face and wiped it dry on his sleeve. He looked about him at the calm atmosphere of the town. Such normality was certainly odd—no gaping apprentices or wide-eyed farmers who had driven in for the occasion. Had Earl Rivers forbidden idle gazing at the young monarch? It seemed unlikely. Rather the Earl would have been more intent on fostering a spirit of devoted loyalty to his nephew than antagonising the townsfolk.

Walter came back, shaking his head in bewilderment. 'The royal party passed through, sir, early this morning, heading for Stony Stratford, it is said.'

'Passed through? His Grace of Gloucester was to meet the King here.'

'Aye, sir.'

'Was any reason given?'

'No. The baker was disappointed. He was hoping to supply the King with special confections baked for the occasion.'

Beaumont rubbed his chin thoughtfully. 'Strange. The Earl must have some good reason for changing his plans at the last moment. Were any innkeepers approached? I imagined the King's lodging would have been prepared in advance.'

'It seems the party passed through hurriedly. Few were present in the streets and the people missed them. The mayor had prepared a special speech of welcome. It's left everyone feeling flat.'

'I can well believe it.'

'Do we go on, sir, or await His Grace of Gloucester?'

'We'll ride on. I have the Duke's messages to deliver.'

The man nodded stolidly but looked back longingly in the direction of an inn doorway which opened invitingly.

Beaumont laughed. 'Come, man, allay your thirst for the present. We'll stop part way betwixt here and Stony Stratford. It will give us a break from the saddle when we sorely need it.'

The soldier sighed but obeyed without argument. Within minutes they had left Northampton and were headed after the royal party.

What sense was there in this new move of Earl Rivers? True Stony Stratford was thirteen miles or so nearer London, but the party would be forced to rest. Heavily laden as Beaumont understood it to be with artillery and baggage wagons piled high with the King's personal belongings from Ludlow, Rivers could not hope now to put a considerable distance between himself and Gloucester. Did he now depend on this race to London? Certainly he who held the King was in a position of power, but for how long could he hold it against the claims of the late King's blood brother and the royal will appointing him guardian?

Walter rode in silent acquiescence. After their short rests their mounts made good speed and when they cantered into a quiet hamlet with its inn boasting a loyal inn sign, 'The Sun of York' Beaumont called a halt and they dismounted for refreshment.

An ostler took their mounts in hand and they pushed into the one room, anxious for the cool trickle of fresh brewed ale down their parched throats.

Three men were seated at a table. They were resting at ease, their ale-jacks well filled, and by no means their first that afternoon by the sound of their relaxed conversation. None of them looked up as Beaumont chose a table nearer to the window and called to the pot-man to bring ale. It would be useless to demand wine in this hostelry. In all events ale would be more welcome after his dusty ride.

Walter downed his first jack without comment and appreciatively wiped his mouth dry on his leathern sleeve. Beaumont drank more sparingly after the first long pull, his thoughts busy with the problems of his mission. He beckoned to the pot-man to bring more ale for his attendant and stretched out his long limbs cramped from the hours in the saddle. He would deliver his messages, see the King then ride back as fast as he could to give Gloucester the news of this further move in the complicated chess game to hold the King and with him the board.

One of the men in the corner guffawed, choked and was soundly smacked on the back by a companion. Another bade him good humouredly to be less of a raw fool.

'Why so?' the first bayed still laughing. 'Is it not meant that we should crow at so easily achieving victory? Look not so grim, man. What comes now of your grave forebodings of trouble with Gloucester's men-at-arms?'

Walter looked up sharply at reference to the Duke's name. One hand spilled ale on to the scrubbed oak table-top. Beaumont leaned forward and placed a warning hand on his wrist. One eyebrow raised bade the man keep silent and a jerk of the chin ordered him to cover his white boar livery with his drab travelling cloak. Beaumont was between him and the little company in the corner. They had not noted him yet. If they remained here discreetly, he might hear more.

'We're not yet in London.'

'Nearer so than My Lord of Gloucester.' The man who'd evidently imbibed too well was under the mellowing influence of ale. Beaumont had to admit that the brew was pleasing. It had undoubtedly loosened the tongue of the mercenary in the corner.

The most cautious of the three exclaimed against his rashness. 'Keep your fools' tongue quiet. Think you the inn-man has blocked ears?'

The other shrugged. 'What matters it to him *what* he hears?'

'I've told you before. Gloucester is well served.'

'In the North, yes. The South was staunch for Edward and will be so for his boy.'

A third voice broke into their bickering. 'We must not stay overlong. The Earl commands our company tonight. We must report to him.'

161

The fellow of the loose tongue appealed to the new voice to back him in his confident declaration. 'Roger, you're over-silent. It's ever been your way,' he chuckled. 'That's perhaps as well. *We* do the talking, you the work, eh man? Will it be like that when we do Rivers's work for him?'

'Silence, you fool.' The second man half rose in his anger and flashed a warning glance towards Beaumont and Walter, seated near the window.

The first man slouched on his stool, scraped its legs harshly against the hard-packed earthen floor and squinted at the newcomers.

'Passing merchant.' He gave judgement on the instant. 'Our business is none of theirs. I've said—'

'You've said enough.' The final speaker's voice competently put an end to their discussions and he called imperatively to the pot-man for their reckoning.

They moved out without further talk, the two less indulgent supporting the more loquacious one between them.

Beaumont did not move until he heard them ride out of the yard then leaned close to Walter's ear.

'What think you of that?'

'Earl Rivers's men.'

'On what business?'

'Bloody business by the sound of it.'

'Aye.' Beaumont tapped one finger

162

thoughtfully against his ale-jack. 'Their words betrayed little, but our drunken friend was close to speaking aloud their victim's name.'

'Hired murderers—you think—'

'I dare not think. What puzzles me is that Rivers is ahead in Stony Stratford. If he intends harm to the Duke, why did he not remain in Northampton? He has the stronger force.'

'True, sir, but he yet guards the King. If the plot should fail—'

Beaumont's pale eyes gleamed. 'Aye, right enough. The man is cunning. He shrugs off the incident and is foresworn. Who would dare accuse him openly of attempting murder? Walter, my lad, I've changed my mind. We must ride back towards the Duke's forces.'

'He'll like as not be in Northampton by this time.'

'Possibly. I think he should have some knowledge of what we overheard. Forewarned is forearmed. In this game the phrase can't be too often repeated.'

It was late in the evening before the two rode again into Northampton to seek the Duke of Gloucester's lodging. Beaumont was flushed with annoyance. His horse cast a shoe on the road and he was forced to seek a smith. The man had promised the work would be done hurriedly and he had decided not to send Walter on ahead alone. It seemed wiser for the two to remain together. There was naught to fear yet. Their acquaintances of 'The Sun of York' had gone on to Stony Stratford to report to Rivers. Yet the work had not been completed efficiently and had taken longer than expected. It was natural he should be irritated by the unfortunate delay. The Duke would now be at dinner, unwilling to give ear to the messages of one of his gentlemen.

There was no time to change and he presented himself at last at Gloucester's lodging to encounter Sir Francis Lovell on the step.

'The Duke is at dinner with his Grace of Buckingham who rode in but an hour or so ago.'

'Buckingham?' Beaumont stopped abruptly and the other frowned.

'It seems his Grace is hot to offer his loyalty. He brings three hundred men. We've had much ado to find them lodgings alongside our own men from Middleham. Did you see the King?'

'No.' Beaumont was conscious of his impatient tone and made a gesture of apology. 'Your pardon, Sir Francis. I have news for the Duke. Will he see me before he retired?'

Lovell shrugged. 'Who knows? My Lord of Buckingham has the greater claim.'

'For all he's married to a Woodville.'

Lovell grunted his approval of Beaumont's sentiments. He had no love for the arrogant, flamboyant Stafford, resplendent in cloth of gold and scarlet despite the need for more

164

discreet apparel at this time of mourning. Buckingham had a glib tongue and Lovell had noted sourly how Gloucester's pale cheeks had flushed with pleasure at sight of his cousin. He was angered with himself that he should grudge Buckingham Richard's favour. Even Beaumont here had recently raised his ire by appearing closer to Richard than he. He was not wont to behave like some jealous female. God's truth, he had loved Dickon all his adult life. That affection was returned, he knew. There was little need for stiffness in greeting Beaumont. He relaxed his tense expression.

'We'll give them some privacy. Later, we'll try to proffer your message, Charles. Let us dine. Ratcliffe is around seeking me. Join us, if you will.'

Beaumont was about to accept but commented on the state of his person, still dusty from the ride when a small company of horsemen clattered into the street and they both looked up, curious to see the late arrivals.

Five men dismounted and approached the inn. Beaumont gave a silent whistle as he recognised the three men he had seen earlier in 'The Sun of York'. Of the two remaining visitors one was unmistakable. The torchlight glinted on the tall figure and clever, pointed features of the Queen's brother, Anthony Woodville, Earl Rivers. The other was younger, not immediately recognised by Beaumont.

Lovell had recovered from his surprise and bowed to the Earl.

Rivers was his pleasant, suavely-spoken self. 'Is the Duke at dinner, Sir Francis? I have ridden hard to greet him.'

'Indeed, sir, we expected you here with the King awaiting us.' Lovell's voice was polite enough but the cool tone reminded the Earl of his duty.

He affected not to notice. 'It seemed that Northampton would be over-full for the comfortable lodging of both our companies. Since we arrived first it seemed sensible to take the King ahead to Stony Stratford. This I would explain to his Grace. May I present my nephew, Sir Richard Grey, the King's half-brother.'

Lovell bowed coolly and stood back to allow the two to precede him into the inn. Rivers could not be kept like a groom awaiting his master.

Beaumont stood irresolute, his head cocked to the three men who'd escorted the Earl and who were now waiting across the courtyard. How soon before they knew him as the merchant briefly seen at the inn? It was imperative they should not see him again in the light until he'd aroused a goodly company to guard the Duke. He misliked this mission. He wrapped his cloak around his body and high to shade his face. He brushed by them to seek the whereabouts of Sir Richard Ratcliffe.

CHAPTER FOURTEEN

Finding Ratcliffe proved more difficult than he had anticipated. Beaumont encountered many of Gloucester's gentlemen in the street and in the inns nearby. None of them seemed sure about Ratcliffe's whereabouts. They were vague in their directions and after the fourth inn Beaumont began to despair. It was imperative that he inform Ratcliffe of Rivers's disloyalty and quickly. Even now the hired assassins would be preparing for their night's work. Soon Gloucester would retire. He was tired from the ride and the day's business. He would be less cautious than normally. It would be all too easy to break into the sleeping chamber and make an end. He cursed the capriciousness of Lady Destiny that she had caused Phoebus, today of all days, to cast her shoe and delay him reaching Gloucester with his warning. Surrounded as the Duke was with friends nearer his own rank it would prove almost impossible for him to force his way in and demand to speak with him.

He crossed the inn-yard and came out into the now almost silent market-place. The members of the household had dispersed to their various lodgings. Irresolute, he stood slapping his hand against his thigh. Where now could he search? Should he order some man-at-arms to make a systematic check of the inns and taverns? It would perhaps be wiser to return to Gloucester's lodging. Surely Ratcliffe would be likely to have his quarters there. On impulse he strode across the cobbles to go back on his tracks. In all events he would be nearer to any threatened danger and forearmed into the bargain. The square seemed quiet at last, though now and then a raucous laugh sounded from the nearby inns. Beaumont slipped on some carelessly discarded vegetable refuse, cursed and bent to recover himself. It was then that he was conscious of the silent shadow behind him. He rose and walked on as unconcerned as ever but now he knew he was recognised. His brain registered the fact that he could now hear two sets of footsteps padding behind him. Which of the three was left at Gloucester's lodging to do the fatal work he could not know, but he must think fast if he were to preserve his own life. As ever the nearness of danger left him ice-cold. His lips twisted wryly. He must walk on as if unaware of his peril. He could, of course, cry for assistance. He was near enough to companions. To do so would alert the third man of the need to hasten in his task. That Beaumont would not risk. He would tackle the two alone if need be, and then secure their companion before causing any commotion.

His hand moved to his sword to ease it in its scabbard. He would not draw yet, but he must be ready. His feet moved on steadily unchanging in rhythm while his eyes searched the darkness ahead. Still the square and street beyond remained deserted. His opponents would not attack here in the open street. They would wait for him to enter some doorway or courtyard, quiet enough for their work. He must deliberately offer them opportunity if he could. As if unaware of their presence he turned into the inn-yard where Phoebus was stabled, paused in the doorway and called for a groom.

'Ho there, ostler.'

There was no answer. It was yet early and the tavern grooms would be taking supper. They deserved it after the wearisome task of coping with the horses of the many nobles who had ridden in with Gloucester.

He cursed aloud and reached for lanthorn and tinder-box, stooping to his task, stumbling somewhat as if tired or over-full of ale.

They were silent, his two followers; he gave them grudging credit for that. He felt them approach him though his ears caught hardly a sound, then his legs were pulled from under him, his head enveloped in some heavy cloth, possibly a riding cloak. He made some show of struggling and attempting to cry out but the sounds were stifled in the thick material, then he lay still as he felt the cold prick of steel at his throat.

'You're sure, he's the man?' The whisper

came hoarsely from the darkness. He couldn't place the voice as a certainty but thought it to be the incautious one who'd blurted out too much in the inn earlier.

The other hushed him and said no words but Beaumont was convinced he gestured in the affirmative. He lay still, his breathing supposedly laboured, waiting. There was no doubt that this could be the end easily enough, if he'd judged his man wrongly.

The man with the dagger laughed aloud then hushed the sound to a half-strangled chuckle at his companion's horrified whisper of protest.

'Make an end, man.' It was clear the other was irritated by his friend's foolhardiness.

'Aye, 'tis ever your way. You've no stomach for the task and ye begrudge me my pleasure in it.'

'I begrudge you nothing, certainly not the rope you'll dangle on if you don't follow my counsel.'

'Softly, softly. Our friend here's in no hurry. He's a right to know why he dies.'

Beaumont made abortive efforts to free himself and his captor laughed again. It was then Beaumont freed his own dagger from his doublet and thrust up straight and true. The man gave a surprised gurgle. His dagger had been deflected upwards by the heaving movement of his own laughter. It scratched downwards harmlessly in the thick material but the man's heavy body fell partially across him.

He'd been a blunderer, too sure of himself, thinking his victim unaware of his own peril. Beaumont's arms had only appeared to be secured, now he pushed upwards freeing himself from the blinding cloth and half crouched, ready for the other man to attack. The lanthorn glowed dully, showing the assassin standing back hard against the doorway. If his dead companion was right, he was less murderously minded but now he would come on for the kill. He *must*, and he *knew* Beaumont was ready for him. There was no element of surprise now. He could take no chances.

Beaumont shouted above the restless stirring of the horses, now whinnying in fear. 'A Gloucester, to me, Beaumont, in the stable.'

The other man gave a snarl of rage, drew his dagger and sped fast along the ground. His own escape was doomed. He might yet end Beaumont and prevent him warning Gloucester's household. His attack might be taken as a personal one or one made for robbery as a thief caught in the act. If die he must, he'd take his accuser with him.

Beaumont read his intention in his eyes in that split second of time. His right leg was pinned under the weight of his dead opponent and he wrenched hard to free himself. He still held his dagger ready but his attacker had the advantage of free movement.

Shouts and slams outside told him he'd been heard. If he could hold off the other, even for minutes, he might yet win through. The man crouched back as if uncertain how to proceed. Beaumont's dagger flicked out like a snake's tongue as a warning. The man's eyes followed its bloodied passage as if hypnotised. His own arm stabbed down towards Beaumont's chest and glanced off his leathern jerkin. Hampered by his trapped leg. Beaumont was unable to retaliate.

Then mercifully the stable was invaded. Three men charged in, stood aghast, then one grabbed for Beaumont's assailant and the other two rushed to his assistance. A groom, blundering in to attend to his restless charges, stood stock-still with shock, then had the presence of mind to help Beaumont move the heavy weight from his leg and thigh.

'Ratcliffe.' Beaumont snapped out the word and attempted to rise. He caught back a yelp of pain, finding his knee badly wrenched in the fall.

A man-at-arms ordered the removal of the prisoner.

'I'll summon him, sir. He's at supper.'

'Gloucester? Has he retired?'

'No, sir, he's yet in the parlour with my lords of Buckingham and Rivers.'

'See to his safety. There's a plot against his life.'

'Aye, sir.' The man called orders to his men

172

and as Beaumont explained the need for a careful search of the premises, listened to his description of the third man he'd seen in the inn.

'Heed Sir Charles Beaumont. Apprehend and keep safe any stranger approaching the inn. Report to Sir Richard Ratcliffe any arrest made. Go carefully. Do not disturb My Lord of Gloucester at meat.'

Ratcliffe signalled Beaumont to remain seated when he entered the tap-room later.

'Rest, man. Your knee still pains you.'

'Did you get him?'

'Aye.'

'Has he confessed?'

Ratcliffe grunted. 'He said nothing, but he will. Give him time.'

He reached for ale, then turned respectfully as Gloucester paused in the doorway before entering. His pale face appeared stern in the light from the candles on the table.

'Are you hurt?' His question was directed at Beaumont who shook his head. Gloucester gestured him to be seated. 'So, you save my life.'

'Sir, I think that an exaggeration of fact. You could have defended yourself well enough, but you were ill-warned.'

'Aye.' Gloucester moved into the room, his hand straying in its customary action to turn the ring on his finger. 'Sir Francis Lovell called me outside the parlour. He informed me of the

173

presence of our two assassins and I believe there were three.'

'There were, sir.'

Ratcliffe stirred uneasily. 'Is My Lord Rivers still in the parlour?'

'Concern yourself not about him, Sir Richard. He is being well entertained by My Lord of Buckingham.'

'For how long, sir?'

Gloucester's eyes met his steadily. He shrugged. 'Till he retired with young Dick Grey.'

'But—'

Gloucester stilled his protest with a wave of his hand. 'Let me finish, Dick. See neither of them leaves Northampton tomorrow.'

Ratcliffe relaxed. At last there was promise of action. 'And you, Your Grace?'

Gloucester moved back to the door. He was smiling, 'I shall return to my guests. See I am called early. I plan to greet My Lord the King before noon in Stony Stratford. See that a strong force accompanies us. It is clear the King needs protection.'

CHAPTER FIFTEEN

Despite the discomfort of his wrenched knee, Beaumont thought his journey to Stony Stratford behind Gloucester and Buckingham well worth the pain it gave him. He watched the greeting between the young King and his uncle with avid interest.

The arrest of Rivers and Grey had been accomplished with little effort. Both men were taken by surprise when they found their way from Northampton barred. Earl Rivers had protested hotly.

Suavely Gloucester informed him that since he feared the assassin's knife and word had been brought to him that only that previous night three hired murderers had been found in the vicinity of the inn, it seemed wiser, for the Earl's own protection, that he was guarded for the time being by Gloucester's men. Rivers's hunted eyes moved from the Protector's bland countenance to Buckingham's mocking gaze. Flamboyant as ever the Duke was handling his mount with studied ease. Rivers looked back at the Protector. This was a changed Gloucester, smiling, quiet but deadly. Rivers knew it and said nothing further. He counselled young Richard Grey to patience and turned his mount to accompany his guards to the town.

Though Richard had left Northampton full early he found that the young King had already left his lodging to Stony Stratford. He compressed his lips in sudden anger and gave the curt order to proceed and overtake the Royal party. Sir Thomas Vaughan and Sir Richard Haute had pressed on in defiance of Gloucester's instructions to meet him here for the ride to London. Beaumont noted his cold fury. Now it seemed clear that Rivers's intention had been to detain him in Northampton, and allow his men to do their work while the young King was hastened on to London.

Gloucester's escort was now strengthened by the addition of three hundred men who had accompanied Harry of Buckingham. Two small detachments Gloucester sent northwards with his prisoners; Rivers to Sheriffs Hutton, young Richard Grey to Middleham. They rode with all speed and soon came in sight of the heavily piled baggage wagons of the King's party. The men-at-arms in their livery displaying the White Boar surrounded Rivers's detachment and though the men from Ludlow far outnumbered them, their officers drew back alarmed at sight of Gloucester's stern-faced men who clearly meant business.

Sir Francis Lovell spurred ahead to halt, Vaughan in the lead with the King. Muttering and giving side-long glances, the company came to a halt and many dismounted. Gloucester rode steadily to the van and at last drew reign some distance from the two traitor knights who sat their mounts, grimly silent, the King between them.

Silently Gloucester dismounted and walked to his nephew's side, dropping to one knee in the roadside to give loyal greeting to his young sovereign.

'Your Grace, I give thanks to God I am in good time to greet you and offer my services and protection on the ride to London.'

The boy was quiet and fidgeted awkwardly with his decorated reins. His tutor, the Bishop of Worcester, rode hastily up to him to remind him of his manners.

'Greet your noble uncle, My Lord. He waits for your permission to rise.'

Edward thrust out his nether lip and peered downwards sulkily. 'We thank you, Uncle Gloucester,' he said coldly. 'Please rise.'

Gloucester rose and came impulsively forward, his arms outstretched to lift the boy from his saddle.

'Ned, lad. It is good to see you well, though this is a sad occasion. It seems long since I saw you. Come let us walk together, you and I.'

The boy drew back his mount, avoiding Gloucester's touch. His horse snorted and stamped backwards, sending up clouds of dust which settled on the Protector's mourning garments. He frowned, his eyes widening at the boy's obvious dislike. He forced himself to be patient, remembering the lad's strangeness. They were near in blood, but distance had meant he had never really known his two nephews. This elder boy had lived his life surrounded by Woodvilles. He would naturally have been under the spell of his Uncle Rivers's natural charm of manner. The Earl's arrest would be a terrible shock.

177

He said quietly, 'Ned, please obey me. I must remind you, you are yet but thirteen and by your father's will in my charge.'

'Where is my Uncle Anthony? *He* cares for me, tells me how to act. I will not submit to you. Why should I?'

'Because I wish it.' The boy's angry blue eyes met his own cool grey ones. They measured each other's worth in that long glance and the blue ones fell. Edward flushed angrily and ungraciously called to Sir Richard Haute to help him dismount.

He was a comely lad, slight and small but with his father's colouring and regality of manner. Even his mourning velvet was elegantly cut and plentifully adorned with jewels. Richard sighed inwardly. The boy seemed effeminate but there were traces of an iron will in the stubborn set of the mouth. His task would not be easy. As he placed a hand on the young shoulder, Edward moodily shrugged it off. Firmly Gloucester gripped his elbow to lead him farther off, where they could talked undisturbed. Before moving he looked up directly at Sir Francis Lovell and made an impatient movement of his free hand. Lovell smiled grimly and nodded, and turned back to the King's gentlemen.

Edward was forced to give way to the gentle but determined pressure on his arm and go with his uncle. He was close to tears.

'You are hurting me,' he cried. 'How dare

you, sir. My Uncle Rivers shall hear of your treatment of me.'

'Earl Rivers is under arrest, sir.'

The King stiffened, his eyes widening in astonishment then darkened with anger.

'He has committed High Treason in taking upon himself the right to govern you, thereby setting aside the will left by your father and the wishes of The Lords in Council. Besides that there are graver accusations which must be investigated. Until a full examination of the evidence has been made I have sent both him and your half-brother, Sir Richard Grey, north.'

The King almost choked with mingled fury and grief. He wrenched at the hand which held him fast and attempted to beat up at Gloucester's breast with his other clenched fist.

Gloucester bent his head and spoke harshly. 'Your Grace will do well to remember your kingly state. To show yourself in a childish rage here will benefit you nothing. My officers have orders to arrest Sir Thomas Vaughan and Sir Richard Haute. You will not aid them by making a scene. Do I make myself clear?'

The King fell back, tears now staining his cheeks, his breath coming in short, angry gasps.

'Do I?' The boy felt his arm shaken, not cruelly, but with sufficient determination to give him pause.

'Yes, My Lord.'

179

Gloucester's stern face relaxed. 'That is well. You have nothing to fear. I shall take you safe to London. You will wish to greet your lady mother, your sisters and your brother of York. Things will seem less frightening once you are home. Come, Ned, will you not trust me? Your royal father loved me well and I him.'

'It seems that I must, sir.'

Gloucester released him with a half sigh. 'That must content me. We will return to Stony Stratford for the night, for there is much to be done. Come greet your cousin of Buckingham. He has come to give you his allegiance. Tomorrow we will ride for London. Your aunt, The Duchess of Gloucester, will soon join us and my own Ned, who is near enough your age. We shall not expect too much of you, yet awhile. You're tired, Ned. In the inn I'll try to explain to you why I've done what I must.'

He turned and found Beaumont regarding him curiously.

'Sir Charles, assist his Grace the King to mount. We return to Stony Stratford.'

CHAPTER SIXTEEN

Meg came to London in the first week of June. The Duchess of Gloucester joined Richard at Crosby Place on the fifth and almost immediately Sir Piers and Lady Langham rode up from Kent with the Clarence children. Beaumont burned to have private words with Meg who was still in attendance on the children, but circumstances appeared to conspire to keep them apart. Beaumont was busy on the Duke's business riding from Westminster to Baynards Castle, where Gloucester spent much time with his mother, Cecily, Dowager Duchess of York, and from there to the Bishop of London's palace where the King lodged and later to the Tower where young Edward was moved in preparation for his coronation true to ancient custom.

The city was quietening down after the alarms and scares of the last days. Gloucester had entered London with the King on May 4th to be greeted loyally and enthusiastically by the people. He found that the Queen with the young Duke of York and her daughters had fled into sanctuary in such haste that a wall had to be hurriedly demolished to admit the free passage of her baggage wagons. Dorset had fled to join her and the news of the arrest of Earl Rivers, Grey and the traitor lords, swept the town. There was no doubt of the citizens' disquiet. Gloucester firmly took control of affairs. Hastings greeted him thankfully and Council meetings were called to discuss future plans. The coronation was fixed for June 22nd. Buckingham raged over the unpredictable behaviour of the Queen.

'What in God's name prompted the woman

181

to act so?' he demanded of Richard. 'Can we not force her to leave Sanctuary or at least to allow young Richard to join his brother? The King frets for him.'

Gloucester counselled patience. 'The Queen fears bogies. Let her stay. She does no harm there. She will emerge in her own good time when she judged the hour ripe.'

'And meanwhile nurses that viper, Dorset, in her bosom.'

'Naturally enough. Dorset is her eldest son. I'll warrant we have little to fear from that quarter. He'll fly the country, that's certain.'

Buckingham grunted. 'Young Richmond will be pleased to receive the support of malcontents.'

Gloucester raised his brows but said nothing. Harry Tudor was still the centre of Lancastrian hopes. He did not fear the association. Dorset would be ill-advised to support a rival claimant to the throne while his half-brother occupied it.

Beaumont had heard that Margaret Woollat was alone in the Duchess's chamber, busy at her embroidery. The Lady Anne had visited her mother-in-law at Baynard's Castle with Lady Langham in attendance. The children had accompanied her and for once Meg was free of her charges. Beaumont lost no time in seeking her.

She rose with a glad cry and he enveloped her in his arms, dusty as he was, having just ridden in from the Duke of Buckingham's lodgings where he'd left messages from the Lord Chamberlain.

'Meg, my love, I'm naught but a messenger boy these days.'

She thrilled to his touch, laughing with pure joy. 'Charles, I have seen you these last two days but only at a distance. I've longed for you to come to me.'

He drew her down on the settle far from the window where prying eyes might intrude on their bliss.

'Well, here I am. How long must I wait, Meg?'

'How long—?' She drew back surprised by his question.

'I've taken a house near The Chepe. It's small but well furnished. You will live finely, my Meg.' He frowned as colour mounted her cheeks and she stammered her distress.

'So soon? Charles—I—'

'Change of heart Meg?' She could not fail to note the sudden chill of his tone.

'No, never that but—'

'But?'

'The children need me. They have come to rely on me, Charles. The Duke proposes to send them to Sheriffs Hutton for a while. He has asked me to take charge for him.'

'But he will release you from service when he knows the need.'

'I know it, my love, but—' she searched for

words to make him understand her dilemma. 'We have all our lives. Just now young Warwick is so distressed, there have been so many fears to face. Time will heal the wounds. Then I can safely leave him to another and while the Duchess is here in London she needs me too. You know her health is not good. The stress of the coming months will not be easy for her.'

He sighed heavily, holding her little hand tight against his cheek for comfort. 'Aye, it is as you say. Now I am hot for you, Meg, I have no patience. The Lord must grant it for I know you are right.'

She nestled against him, her free hand reaching up in her characteristic gesture, to his lips. 'It will not seem long. The days will soon pass and we shall have moments like this.'

'Few enough while—' He broke off abruptly as the door was unceremoniously jerked open and Sir Richard Ratcliffe entered.

'I'm sorry, Charles.' He waved one hand apologetically as Beaumont sprang to his feet in anger. 'I would not have disturbed you for I knew the circumstances. Gloucester has returned from the Council Meeting. He demands your presence instantly.'

Meg stood up and touched Beaumont's arm beseechingly. 'Go, my love. You cannot keep his Grace waiting.'

Outside, Ratcliffe lowered his voice as he kept pace with Beaumont's angry strides. 'He's in a rare fury. What occurred at the Tower, God only knows.'

Beaumont halted. 'Then why does he send for me?'

Ratcliffe shrugged. 'Think you one of his messages went astray?'

'Not by my carelessness.' Beaumont straightened his shoulders. 'Well, let us discover our sins.'

Gloucester had his back to the room as Beaumont entered on his command and bowed low. The Duke did not turn and Beaumont waited uneasily as Ratcliffe withdrew. When Gloucester swung round, Beaumont saw at once that Ratcliffe had spoken truly. The mouth was held in a hard line, the grey eyes blazed with anger.

'Sir Charles, you swore to me in York you would never repeat the information you gave me then in private.'

Beaumont's eyes widened. 'My Lord, I did not.'

'Say you so? Then know that today the Bishop of Bath and Wells repeated the story in full Council before I was aware of his intentions and so that it was impossible to prevent him.'

Beaumont's lips tightened involuntarily. 'You give me the lie, sir? I repeat, I have spoken to no one.' His eyes did not fall under Gloucester's scrutiny and the Duke made a sudden exclamation and turned from him to a chair.

'Forgive me, Charles. I am too angry to think clearly. Sit, man.' He sank down in the chair while his hand beat a quick tattoo on the polished oak table-top.

'My Lord, may I know what occurred?'

'Surely, Dr Stillington requested permission to address the Council. We were busy but the matter seemed urgent, I thought some trifling fault in the coronation arrangements, possibly a slight the man fancied levelled at himself. He seemed excited, almost hysterical. After asking me leave to speak he blurted out the truth of the tale. It seems he was responsible for the betrothal contract, my brother pledging him to silence. Now I recall Stillington was imprisoned by Ned when George—' he hesitated and Beaumont nodded silently. 'He claimed the matter had weighed heavily on his conscience, that now before the sacred oil was placed on the young Edward he must speak. We could not in honour crown a bastard King of England.'

'Sir, why did you doubt me?' Beaumont's question was direct.

'The man has kept silent long enough. Why does he choose now to speak?'

'Before, he was afraid, sir.'

'True.' Gloucester broke off his impatient tapping and twisted the ring on his finger, now more thoughtful than angry. 'Yet still he stirs a hornets' nest. Someone persuaded him to talk.'

'I understand your lady mother knew of the betrothal.'

Gloucester looked up quickly then shook his head. 'I think—she would not, at least without consulting me.'

'She has not spoken of what she knew?'

'No. Had she the intention of revealing it, she would have done so before this.'

'My Lord Hastings?'

'No. The man was stunned. Had he known he would have murdered Stillington before allowing him to so slander Ned's children.'

'My Lord of Buckingham?'

There was a pause. Again Gloucester frowned at Beaumont. 'It is possible. Who knows what fancies lie in Harry's mind? He was present and not displeased by the news, but how would he know when Hastings did not?'

'My Lord, there must be many who knew, those present at the ceremony. Stillington was the priest. There were altar boys, singing boys. From one such lad the Duke of Clarence heard the tale.'

'Aye, and dear it cost him.'

'You do not now question the truth of it?'

'No.'

Beaumont stirred uncomfortably at the heavy sigh. The Duke rose and went to the window. 'Summon my secretary. I do not like the air of London. Today's news has torn apart the peace I thought had come. We'll have

187

reinforcements, Charles, from York where I can trust my own men of the north.'

'Shall I ride for you, sir?'

Gloucester's voice was muffled oddly. 'No, I prefer you here by my side with Sir Francis Lovell. Sir Richard Ratcliffe will go for me and to my cousin Neville. Meanwhile leave me, Charles.'

In the doorway Beaumont paused. 'What happens now, Your Grace?'

'I wish I knew. The answer lies in God's hands. I must leave it with him.'

CHAPTER SEVENTEEN

Beaumont leaned forward to touch gently Meg's hand as she sat in the darkening parlour of 'The Golden Cockerel'. Jake Garnet had left them for a while to attend some customer when Bess had called urgently. He had been stunned by the news and had said so bluntly when Beaumont had taken Meg to dine there two days later. Meg's own heart had been sorely torn. She had known the late King's children, the elder boy scarcely at all, but the little Duke of York has been a special a favourite during the time she had spent as sewing woman to The Lady Elizabeth. Like all others they met she could scarce believe the truth of the matter. It was still not common

188

gossip in the city but those at court had heard from the Lords present at that fatal meeting and Beaumont had not sought to keep the facts from Meg.

Jake Garnet had been direct. 'What then is the Duke's intention, Sir Charles? Will he seek to overset the boys?'

'Can it be doubted?' Beaumont said quietly. 'The lawyers even now wrangle. The King wed The Lady Elizabeth Grey before Lady Eleanor Butler died. The marriage was no true one and no law in England can legitimatise the King's children.'

'Then the crown will go to the Duke of Clarence's son?'

'He is attainted. The boy is delicate, unfit to rule.'

'And you think the Duke of Gloucester will take the crown?'

Beaumont was angered by the stolid bluntness of the other.

'Who knows what he will do? He is truly England's heir. Can you doubt his right to reign or his ability?'

'There will be many who will speak ill of him.'

'And you, Jake Garnet, will you?'

Garnet grunted. 'It is ill to see the late King's children stood aside.'

'Gloucester knows that well enough. The boy is proud. He will not take the shame lightly.'

189

'Does Gloucester want the crown?'

Beaumont glared back at the innkeeper's kindly face, now grave with concern.

'If he does, I for one will not blame him. England needs a strong King. You yourself feared a minority. Can you deny it?'

'Nay, I'll not do that. God defend us from the wars again.'

'Then pray he *does* accept the crown. Gloucester alone can hold the lords in check.'

Meg had remained silent during this exchange and now that they were alone she said quietly, ' 'Tis said that Earl Rivers and Sir Richard Grey are to be arraigned for treason, Charles. Think you Richard intends to remove his other uncle from the boy?'

'Yes, Meg. I know the truth of that. Rivers planned Gloucester's death in Northampton because he feared this news would break.'

'Earl Rivers? I cannot believe this of him. He is a kind man and charming—'

'But desperate to save a crown, my Meg. A man stakes high when he gambles for a throne. Believe me, I know.'

They were silent after this and sat for a spell in the peace of the quiet parlour. Afterwards he pleaded with her to visit the small house he'd bought for their retreat. She shook her head at him gently but in the end consented and he called to Jake for their reckoning and they walked the short distance, the night being fine.

Despite a momentary hanging back as he

unlocked the door, once over her reluctance, she ran all over the little house exploring eagerly and giving little cries of delight.

'Oh, Charles, it's beautiful and you've chosen the furnishings and hangings with such loving care.'

He drew her close and whispered against her cheek. 'The house is pleasant enough. It will not be beautiful until you live in it.'

'Soon, Charles, I promise.'

'Aye, love, I know. I'll wait patiently though it breaks my heart.'

'Gloucester will need you now, as The Lady Anne needs me.'

'He'll need every good man he has. Praise God, Langham has come up from Kent. Gloucester will ever be able to rely on Ratcliffe and Lovell.'

'And Sir Charles Beaumont?'

'Aye.'

He led her out at last and he turned just once and gave the house on lingering look before re-locking it and taking her arm to escort her back to Crosby Place. It was getting late now and they would be missed. Instinctively they quickened their steps. Suddenly Meg gave an exclamation of surprise, a little indrawn breath and drew back as if for his protection.

'Mistress Shore, leaving her husband's house. Stay back, Charles. I would rather she did not see me.'

He frowned as he watched the cloaked figure

191

hurry round the corner and head back towards the Sanctuary of Westminster. 'Does she now associate with the Queen? I had thought that unlikely.'

Meg nodded. 'They have never seemed enemies, though rivals in the King's bed. Why do you start, Charles?'

'I know the man with her, Sir William Norris. Strange, I had not thought to find him in such company. He is Hastings's man. We were ever at each other's throats before Barnet and Tewkesbury.'

'Hastings's man?' She stopped and peered after the two hurrying figures. 'Do you say so? I have seen him with My Lord Marquess of Dorset.'

In the gloom she saw the well-known glitter of Beaumont's light eyes. 'Dorset?'

'He was in attendance on Dorset at Middleham and later when I was in service to The Lady Elizabeth.'

'He keeps Woodville company does our friend, Norris?' He put out one hand and drew her gently into the shadows. 'Meg, you once said Dorset aimed high for our fair Jane's favours.'

'I'm sure of it. The Queen warned him once in my hearing not to antagonise the King.'

'Yet I found our Jane in Hastings's apartments some days after the King's death.'

'But it is well known now among his intimates that Jane Shore is My Lord

Hastings's mistress. I understand he has always loved her. 'Tis said it was Lord Hastings who first took the King to Shore's shop and lost her to his master.'

'What think you of Jane Shore, Meg?'

She shrugged. 'One could know Mistress Shore for years and never think what she would do next. She was never friendly towards me. I was beneath her notice.'

'Was there any indication that she returned Dorset's tender feelings?'

She hesitated but only for a moment. Even in the dusk he could tell she had blushed hotly. 'Dorset is—very handsome. I think Mistress Shore—well he is younger than My Lord Hastings or even His Grace the King—she—'

'Exactly, that is what I'm thinking. But if she favours Dorset why now does she seek Hastings's attentions?'

'Dorset is disgraced. He must fly abroad if he is to save his life—'

'And Norris was his man. H'm.' He considered. 'Hastings will not be pleased by the turn events have taken. He had thought to see Edward's son crowned. Now—who knows?'

'But he would not offer his allegiance to his old enemies the Woodvilles. Why, did he not lie imprisoned by word of the Queen?'

Beaumont grinned mirthlessly. 'He did, but so was I banished by the King and was no favourite of Gloucester. Indeed, I served him ill on more than one occasion. We all change our loyalty when it is to our advantage. I think it unwise of Gloucester to trust the Lord Chamberlain too well.' He gave a glance back towards the street from which Mistress Jane Shore had emerged. 'Now why should she visit her old home? To meet someone in a place none would expect her to go? It is a possibility.'

'But she is openly with Hastings.'

'But not with Dorset. I confess I am puzzled, Meg, but I do not like the game. Come, let us go home.'

The Duchess was anxious to retire when they reached Crosby Place and Meg sped to attend her and to see the children settled. Beaumont sought out Sir Francis Lovell to enquire if he were needed further that night.

Lovell was resting in the hall after a gruelling day at Gloucester's side. 'His Grace should rest,' he said dourly as Beaumont sank down beside him and reached for the cup Lovell pushed towards him. 'He hardly has time to sleep let alone see his wife and child, these days.'

'He is with his secretary?'

'He's closeted with Catesby.'

'Hastings's man.'

'Yes. He arrived an hour back in some haste. I was anxious to put him off till tomorrow but Richard insisted on seeing the man.'

'Some urgent message from the Lord Chamberlain perhaps. Is there not another Council meeting at the Tower tomorrow?'

Lovell growled an assent, poured wine for Beaumont and drunk deep himself.

'Meetings, secret conclaves! I wish we were back in the north. The very air of London seems poisoned with more than the plague. If Gloucester takes my advice he'll force the Queen to hand the Duke of York into his custody and make his own peace in the city.'

Beaumont sat back and gazed ruminatively at the ceiling. 'I think it will be long before Gloucester and his Lady see Middleham again,' he said quietly.

'That's certain and sure as fate if he stays, I stay with him.' Lovell smiled as Beaumont stretched lazily.

'I'll to bed, unless I'm needed.' Beaumont rose and paused before leaving the hall. 'Sir Francis, before the Duke leaves for the Tower tomorrow ask if I might see him.'

The other nodded briefly and Beaumont left him.

He was summoned early the following morning to Gloucester's bed-chamber to find the Duke completing his dressing.

'Come, Charles, Frank tells me you wish to see me. Be brief. I am expected at the Council meeting by nine o'clock.'

Lovell shrugged expressively over Gloucester's shoulder and, at a gesture of dismissal, bowed and went out of the room.

'Well?' The Duke was impatient.

Quietly Beaumont related his experience of

195

the previous night. He found Gloucester attentive. He put on his rings, adjusted his gold chain and sat quietly until the end, then he nodded thoughtfully.

'You were wise to mention the matter. There may be nothing to disturb us. I had not known Mistress Shore was connected with the Marquess of Dorset. That is interesting—very interesting. You attend me, Charles?'

'I would be pleased to if you wish, sir.'

'Do so.' Gloucester rose and called to Lovell. The interview was at an end. Beaumont stood back respectfully.

The Duke was welcomed at the Tower by Lord Hastings and conveyed immediately to the Council chamber where Bishop Morton, the Duke of Buckingham and Lord Stanley awaited him. Beaumont, with Lovell, stood guard in the corridor. Lovell said little but he seemed uneasy. Beaumont pursed his lips as he noted they had been escorted by a troop of the Duke's own men who stood stolidly watchful in the courtyard.

'The Duke seems cheerful today.' Beaumont lounged on a bench and smiled at Lovell.

Lovell started as if surprised that he was there then apologised and nodded.

'Aye—but then I think it is forced.'

'You believe so?'

'I know my Dickon well. Something disturbed him last night—something Catesby said, damn the man. Did he grant your favour?'

'Favour? No, I asked for nothing. I had some information—' he trailed off uncertainly as Lovell's frown deepened.

'Intrigue and more intrigue, as I said.'

'You'd have the Duke well warned?'

'I'd have him at peace.'

'There's more ways than one of obtaining that state.' Beaumont's tone was grim.

Lovell's angry stare challenged him to reveal himself but he turned away. They both fell silent, each moodily aware of the other's irritation, Beaumont to play with the hilt of his dagger, Lovell to pace the corridor restlessly. Sounds of altercation from the courtyard brought both to attention in an instant.

William Catesby burst into the corridor followed by the captain of Gloucester's company.

'The Duke is in the council chamber?' He flung this question at Lovell.

'The meeting has gone on for some time.'

'I must speak with him urgently.'

'Catesby, you forget yourself—'

'Sir Francis, the Duke himself commanded my presence this morning. Unfortunately I was delayed. Please—'

Lovell hesitated. To break into Council was no easy task. He sighed. These days his life had become increasingly difficult. He tapped upon the door and was admitted after a whispered discussion with a page in attendance.

Gloucester came out at once, took Catesby's arm and led him off along the corridor. They stood together out of earshot of both Beaumont and Lovell who had returned to stand by his side breathing heavily.

'Frank.' Gloucester called urgently and Lovell hurried to his side.

When all three returned to the doorway Beaumont noted that all the blood had drained from Gloucester's face. He stumbled and would have fallen awkwardly had not Lovell put out an arm to support him.

'Charles,' he said quietly, 'attend me in the chamber please but first summon my guard from the courtyard.'

'Yes, sir.' Beaumont obeyed Lovell's urgent signal and half-walked half-ran on his errand.

He was never to forget the events of the next moments. He came up sharp in the doorway, the captain following fast on his heels, to hear Gloucester's cold, biting words of accusation.

'Understand, My Lord Hastings, you are hopelessly implicated. Yesterday I refused to believe your accuser. Now I have direct proof. That whore Jane Shore carried messages between you and Dorset. With My Lord Stanley here, whose wife has meddled in his affairs once too often, and Bishop Morton you have plotted to take my life.'

Stanley let out a torrent of words, angry, meaningless, and Gloucester silenced him with one look of scorn.

Morton sat still, a smile curving the corners of his finely chiselled lips. Buckingham was seemingly appalled by the accusation levelled at The Lord Chamberlain. Hastings stood white-face, too thunder-struck to answer.

'Will, I trusted you.' Gloucester's voice was pleading. 'You of all men. I was unwilling to accept this. You say nothing. God, man, speak. Your life is at stake.'

'You know too much, Richard. It would be useless.' Hastings sounded tired and anxious to end a discussion which would prove fruitless.

Gloucester went to him. Hastings turned his head, unwilling to face the direct stare of those grey eyes.

'Can you be such a fool, Will, as to bring yourself to this for such a woman as Jane Shore?'

Hastings swung round and for a moment his eye flashed sudden fire, then he raised one hand to dash against his eyes. 'Do not speak her name, Your Grace,' he said huskily. 'Think what you will. I have no regrets.'

'You deny nothing?'

Hastings shook his head again once. Gloucester turned to Morton who continued to remain unperturbed. Stanley had been forced back against the wall by two sturdy archers. He had given up the attempt to bluster his way out of the affair.

'Bishop Morton, what have you so say in answer to this charge?' Gloucester eyed the prelate coldly.

'Nothing, My Lord. At this stage of the proceedings I think it fitting for me to hold my tongue. Doubtless, My Lord of Gloucester, you will, in good time, bring ample proof of your accusations?' His tone was silky. He raised one arm deliberately and adjusted the set of his sleeve.

'Take My Lord Hastings away.' Gloucester moved aside as if to avoid further contact with his old comrade-at-arms. 'Make your peace with God, Will,' he said quietly, 'it is the only counsel I can give you now. I will send you a priest.'

Hastings inclined his head. He made no remonstrance when his guards led him away, but went with them as if willingly. At the door he bent his head to whisper in Lovell's ear. Sir Francis listened then straightened up and preceded his prisoner down the length of the corridor.

Gloucester seated himself wearily and indicated that Buckingham was to remain with him.

'Rest yourself, Harry. Captain, hold my Lord Stanley and the Bishop in close arrest until I give further orders concerning them. Charles, stay with us by the door. Two men remain on guard outside. Give me a moment to rest then send Catesby to join us.'

Beaumont gave the orders then returned to his post, his back to the door of the council chamber.

Buckingham passed a hand over his sweating forehead. 'They intended harm to both of us?'

Gloucester grinned. 'Aye, Harry, you were to form part of the sacrifice.'

'When did you know?'

'The details, final proof—not until this morning. Catesby came with some tale last night. I could not accept it. Now, I must. Stanley's men were intercepted by mine as they moved towards the Tower.' He glanced across at Beaumont. 'You filled in one part of the puzzle when you spoke of Jane Shore's meeting with Norris. Hastings had thrown in his hand with Dorset. I had the whole of it then and proof Catesby brought me later.'

'Stanley, too? I always believed the man craven—'

'As I said, Harry, Stanley is ruled by his wife. Because of that, I'll not act against the man.'

Buckingham slammed a hand palm down against the table. 'Richard, Stanley must die.'

'No, Harry.' Gloucester's tone was quiet but firm. 'There's been enough blood letting and there'll be more. Rivers, Grey, Will Hastings.' He sighed and considered a document under his hand. 'Morton I'll entrust to your care. Bury that intriguing personality of his on your estates out of harm's way for a while.'

'If you wish it.'

'I do.'

Buckingham grunted as Gloucester's quill moved steadily over the parchment. 'What fools men make of themselves over women. That harlot Shore must answer to God for her hand in this affair.'

'I will commit her to close arrest for a spell. The church must be her accuser. Too long she has flaunted herself, a known adulteress. It is time she did public penance. That way her admirers will have less confidence in her.' He paused in his writing though he did not look up. 'The sentence is more merciful than she deserves. She has Will's blood on her conscience.' He signed his name then put down the quill and rose as Catesby entered and bowed.

'Attend me at Crosby Place later, Catesby. I'll have work for you. Know you have my gratitude.' As Catesby lifted his eyes he met those of Gloucester's. Perhaps he read in them something which disturbed him for his own expression clouded. As if aware of Catesby's doubts Gloucester smiled, that rare smile Beaumont knew and recognised. Catesby's face flushed with the joy of acceptance. Gloucester pulled on his gloves and resumed his brisk business-like manner.

'May we see you at dinner, My Lord of Buckingham? Her Grace has missed you these last days. I shall find pleasure in your company. Charles, I am ready to leave.'

Beaumont opened the door and bowed as

Gloucester withdrew. As he straightened he caught Buckingham's expression. The eyes were puzzled and he tapped one finger against the document Gloucester had left for Council's attention. He glanced after the Duke then down at the signature. Catesby, turning in that moment, caught the look. He smiled uncertainly as though the two exchanged some unspoken communication of ideas, then Buckingham caught Beaumont's questioning stare and met it frostily.

Beaumont did not lower his eyes. It was never his way to admit superiority in any save the Duke. He bowed coldly to both men and followed in Gloucester's wake. Nevertheless he was frowning when he reached the courtyard. Buckingham was right. Both Stanley and Morton needed to be silenced permanently. Gloucester was too trusting. He offered his favours now openly to these men but was he wise? Beaumont shrugged as he mounted and cantered out of the gate. Lovell was sensible to be uneasy. It would pay him, Beaumont, to watch everyone, even Lovell.

CHAPTER EIGHTEEN

Though he had made every effort to be with Meg, Beaumont found during the next dew days he saw little of her. He was in constant attendance on Gloucester whom indeed it was no longer safe to leave unattended by at least two or three of his trusted gentlemen. The Duke became more and more taciturn and indrawn as day followed day. It was obvious he felt Hastings's death very deeply though he made no further reference to the Lord Chamberlain's treachery. Since all his property and estates were confiscate to the Crown, Gloucester immediately wrote to his widow assuring her that her property would be restored to her and that she should lack for nothing. Without a qualm he signed the death warrants of Earl Rivers and Sir Richard Grey who were condemned in the north.

It seemed to Beaumont now that Meg was deliberately avoiding him. He saw her only hurriedly in hall where she made sure they were surrounded by others, or if he encountered her during the day, she made an excuse to leave him. The Duchess needed her to match some silks or the children would miss her if she stayed too long away from them. Always he found it impossible to speak what was in his heart. Anger burned in him at her refusal to tell him of what ailed her and he determined that such a state of affairs could not be allowed to continue.

With this in mind he dispatched a page to the Duchess's apartments where he knew Meg was in attendance to ask formal permission for her absence. He knew well enough Anne would gladly grant the favour and Meg would be forced to come out to him. The corridor was empty, the pages gossiping in the courtyard, there would be some minutes at least for them to talk together in private.

The swish of her skirts told him of her presence. The page who had carried his message looked at them curiously and Beaumont curtly dismissed him.

'What is it?' she said, her colour heightened. 'You shame me to ask the Duchess for speech alone with me.'

'Is this what you now consider, my Meg? Our time together— something shameful.'

Her blush deepened. 'Well no—I mean you embarrass me. Is something wrong?'

'That is what I wish to know from you, Meg.' He was gentle but determined.

'Of course not. What do you mean?'

'You have ceased to love me?'

'You know that is not true.'

'But you have avoided me.'

'I've been busy. We both have been—'

'Not too busy to talk.'

She bit her lip at his insistence. 'Of what should we talk? The court does nothing else.'

'What does the court say, Meg?'

'Nothing of consequence. You know ladies-in-waiting and pages. I—'

'What has been said to alarm you?'

She turned from him now, close to tears. He waited and suddenly she came back and clutched at his fingers urgently. 'Take me away. Please take me away. I'm afraid—'

'Of what, Meg?'

'For the children.'

'For the *children*?' He echoed her words, doubt making his tone harsh. 'What should happen to the children?'

'Now he has both of them. The little Duke of York is in the Tower with his brother. What is to prevent the Duke disposing of them?'

'Meg, do I hear you correctly?' He tore her fingers downwards and held them tight within his own. As she was silent but for a choked sob he shook them. 'Did you hear me? Are you saying Gloucester is capable of murder? Let us not be afraid of the term. If that is in your thoughts let it out, Meg. Be honest with me and yourself.'

She was crying now quietly. 'It is what they are saying. Why else should My Lords of Buckingham and Gloucester send the Archbishop of Canterbury to the Sanctuary to demand the Duke of York's person?'

'Perhaps he thinks as you do. He is anxious to secure their safety.'

'He would fear for the Duke of York's person left in the safe keeping of his own mother?'

His expression was grave and he weighted his words before answering her. 'Elizabeth Woodville needs her sons as pawns in the chess-game of power. While she held young

York she could gather malcontents around her. Dorset is in France. He intrigues with Richmond. Why, think you, does he do that? Richmond's claim is through the Lancastrian line. Would he be prepared to give his allegiance to Edward's sons?'

She stared at him doubtfully and he touched her cold cheek lightly with one finger. 'If Elizabeth throws in her hand with Richmond it could only be because she intended to play one of her daughters as chief pawn.'

'And sacrifice the boys?' Meg's whisper was incredulous.

He shrugged. 'Who knows, my Meg? I've learned to trust few men. Gloucester is one of them. He will do what he can for the children, of that I am sure.'

'The King dislikes him.' Meg considered thoughtfully. She had been to the Tower to visit the boys twice with the Duchess of Gloucester and several times on her own with the Duke's authority. She had known the younger prince and played with him when she'd been in the Lady Elizabeth's household. Now he welcomed her gladly, as an old friend. 'Little Richard is less haughty, more amenable. He is prepared to accept his uncle's authority. Given time there would be genuine affection between them.'

'Then what have you to fear?'

'There have been rumours, Charles, ugly—terrible.'

'I know.' Charles tightened his lips angrily. 'It is to Richmond's advantage that the realm should doubt The Lord Protector. Heed them no more.'

She smiled at last, the old warmth lighting up her face. 'Oh, Charles, I'm sorry. So much has happened lately and I feared—'

'You must allow nothing to part us, Meg.' He took both her hands prisoner and raised them to his lips. He felt her whole body tremble and he expelled a sigh of thankfulness. Meg was his, all his. He did not need to fear. Soon—soon now he would—

There was an urgent call down the corridor, a patter of feet, a woman's feet running hard, not the dignified slop of soft leather on the stone floor he was accustomed to hear. Meg tore her hands from his grasp as Lady Alicia Langham appeared at the bend of the passage.

'Meg, Meg Woollat, come quickly—The Duchess is taken ill.' She halted abruptly at sight of Beaumont. 'Sir Charles, come and help me carry her to her chamber, I've dispatched a page for a physician.'

He followed her hurriedly into the Duchess's apartment. Anne of Gloucester was huddled in her chair, her embroidery frame hastily dashed aside. She was helpless, caught in a paroxysm of coughing. Blood stained her white kerchief she held to her lips and had splashed on to the rich golden silk of her kirtle. She had haemorrhaged from the lungs, that was plain.

Still the harsh cough rended her slight form. Beaumont lifted her in strong arms and carried her through to her chamber.

A bevy of frightened maids started up at his entrance. Alicia dismissed them curtly, sending one for a basin of scented water and towels and forbidding the others to return. Meg had stacked up the pillows on the bed and gently Beaumont laid the sick woman against them that she might breathe more easily. He withdrew to the foot of the bed while Meg poured water for her mistress and Alicia took charge at the door, snatching the bowl and towels from the returning lady-in-waiting and coming to her former mistress's side to bathe Anne's forehead, hands and throat. Meg removed the cumbersome hennin with its stiff wire and gauzy veil and the Duchess's golden hair tumbled in a soft cloud on to her shoulders.

Beaumont waited for the bout to pass. He was grim-faced. This was not unexpected. He had watched the little Duchess fade and wilt under the stresses of the last weeks. She should be away from all this, back in Middleham secure from the intrigues, rumours, cruelties of Westminster. He knew she would not leave Richard—not now while he needed her. And he did, that was clear enough.

She stopped coughing at last and gently waved away Alicia's ministrations. Two hectic spots burned in her pale cheeks and she had scarcely breath enough to talk.

'Alicia, keep my boy away. He worries when he sees me like this. Will you go to him?'

'But—'

'Meg will stay with me till the physician has been. Please, my dear—'

Alicia stooped and kissed her hand. She kept her head averted as she left the room, but Charles suspected that tears gleamed in her dark eyes.

Anne gestured him forward as he muttered his intention of withdrawing. 'Come closer, Sir Charles. I would speak with you.'

'Lady, you must not talk. Rest yourself.'

'Richard is at Baynards Castle. He visits his Lady Mother.'

'I'll ride and bring him home to you.'

She made as if to speak then coughed weakly again. He frowned as he watched her frail shoulders shaken once more by the tearing coughs. Meg shook her head at him from the opposite side of the bed.

'Duke Richard must be told his lady is worse. Go quickly Charles.'

'No.' Anne conquered the coughing bout and arrested him as he reached the door. She was spent and panting for breath. 'Do not alarm him.'

'Lady, he must know. He would censure us all if we kept this from him.'

'He will send me back to the north and I'll not go—not yet. Later when all this is over.'

210

He turned from her suddenly embarrassed by the knowledge which made her hope impossible. He had returned to her side and she reached out and touched his arm.

'He is not safe here in London. We shall go, in time.' Her tone was wistful. As he made no reply she said more clearly this time, 'They will make him stay, Norfolk, Buckingham and the rest.'

'England needs him, Lady.'

'*We* need him, Sir Charles, my son and I.'

Meg hurried to the door as a knock suggested that the Duchess's physician had come at her anguished summons. Meg ushered him in, a tall figure in black furred robe. He tutted his alarm at his patient's state.

'Your Grace has not heeded my warnings. You overtalk your strength. The Duke will hold me to account.'

Anne waved to Beaumont to withdraw and Meg went with him to the door.

'Prepare him for the seriousness of her condition. He has been with her little of late.'

'Affairs have given him little time.'

She nodded. '*Will* he take the crown, Charles? Is this what you wish?'

He squeezed her fingers. 'How else will England remain at peace? Who but Gloucester can keep it so?'

'But the Duchess—'

He looked back at the closed door. 'She knows well enough how ill she is. They have

211

both known for a long time.'

Alarm grew in her eyes. 'She will die?'

'I pray God it may be some time yet. I'll go to the Duke. I wish I could take him happier news.'

Deciding it would be swifter to walk than wait while his horse was saddled, he hurried out into the London streets. Near Baynards Castle his way was barred by excited crowds. The situation was by no means new to him. These last weeks had seen crowds gather day after day for some new event. He pressed his way through, at first good-humouredly, later with more determination. At the gate of the castle he was stayed by the guard, then allowed into the courtyard. Here Catesby met him as he made to enter the castle. The man's whole being glowed with an exhilaration Beaumont had not suspected lay in his nature.

'He has accepted the crown. It is done at last. Praise God. England will lie at peace again.'

Beaumont stopped dead in his tracks. 'Gloucester has been offered the throne, you say?'

'Aye, by a deputation led by the Lord Mayor. My Lord of Buckingham led the deputation into the Duke's presence. I heard it all. They pleaded with him on bent knees for the well-being of the realm. He was hesitant. Never have I seen him so pale, but controlled, as calm as ever.'

'Then Gloucester will be King?'

'Aye, the third Richard to reign in Westminster.'

'Westminster, truly, as you say. The north will see him now but rarely.'

Catesby checked at the graveness of Beaumont's tone. 'You sound distressed. Does not the news please you?'

'It does, Sir William. None is more thankful than I that Gloucester should be King.'

'Then what ails you, man?'

'A personal problem, naught else.'

Catesby shrugged then excused himself and went about his business.

It was some time before Beaumont was at last ushered into the Duke's presence. He went down on one knee in due reverence. Gloucester smiled thinly as he extended his hand for the other's kiss of greeting.

'You have heard then?'

'I have, sir.'

'I know I can rely on your loyalty.'

Beaumont made no reply and the Duke smiled again.

'I spoke once of your ambition, Sir Charles. I shall not forget.'

'I did not come to remind you of such a moment, sir.' Beaumont hesitated as Gloucester's grey eyes looked into his own directly. There was no way to soften a blow such as this. 'Your lady is sick, sir. I came to warn you.'

Only for a moment Gloucester's face

betrayed his agonizing fear.

'How bad is it?'

'The physician is with her—she is bleeding from the lungs. She has exhausted herself.'

Gloucester rose at once. 'I'll go to her.' He sighed. 'This news will bring no comfort to Anne. She longs for the peace of Middleham.' One eyebrow quirked upwards as he caught Beaumont's look of interrogation. 'You wonder about my feelings? They are mixed, Sir Charles, as always, at such a time as this. Anne knows well enough the need which keeps me here. We have faced this in the past, though neither of us has spoken of it. Let us go, take leave of my Lady Mother.'

CHAPTER NINETEEN

The August sun lit Warwick Castle with its splendour as Beaumont paced in its garden with Meg by his side.

'The Queen is more rested today,' he said quietly. 'There is more colour in her cheeks. Progress has been too much for her, yet she proves me wrong. She was laughing just now. We've heard little of that during her illness these last few weeks.'

'We are heading north.' Meg paused to pick a rose and ran her fingers warily over its thorned stem, then lovingly over the scented petals.

Beaumont took it from her. 'You chose unwisely—a scarlet rose, my Meg.' He carefully extracted the thorns and gave it back to her. She was dreamily content and paused on the grassy slope, her eyes half-closed against the sun.

'Scarlet or white, what does it matter? Both are beautiful.'

He smiled at her womanly unconcern. 'Now that she *is* better, you will think over what I said?' He frowned as she still appeared to be wrapped in her own thoughts. She nodded, yet he was not satisfied. Indeed he felt she had not attended to what he had said. He reached out to force her attention but she was too quick for him and gathering up her skirts turned back to the rose arbour.

He cursed beneath his breath and followed more slowly. Today was one of the few occasions he had found it possible to excuse himself from his duties close to the person of the King, since that day in Baynards Castle when he'd faced Richard with the news of his wife's sickness only minutes after he had accepted the throne.

She *had* recovered though not entirely. Beaumont could recollect the sight of her even now on that day when she'd paced slowly beside her husband, pale but every inch a queen, weighted down by the robes of sovereignty, her train carried for her by Lady

Stanley. Beaumont's lips twisted wryly at the irony of the circumstance. That haughty dame had betrayed no hint, on that occasion, of her seething hatred for the new King and his Consort. It had been a glorious ceremony, the Abbey packed with the lords of Yorkist and Lancastrian factions. Richard had made it clear enough he bore malice towards none. All who rendered him true allegiance were welcome at the solemn ritual and afterwards in Westminster Hall for the feasting which followed the coronation. The Abbey Church had rung loud enough with the loyal acclamation which answered the Bishop's question. 'God save the King.' Praise God he *was* King indeed, crowned and touched with holy oil. Who now would attempt to put aside the Lord's annointed? Even here, in Warwick, Beaumont sighed in answer to his own question.

Richard had done ill to leave the capital. London still ran with gossip, remarks, whispers. Talk such as this was natural enough. Jake Garnet of 'The Golden Cockerel' had made it clear his sympathies still lay with Edward's rejected sons in the Tower. Beaumont knew that London was staunchly for King Richard but he needed to be there in his palace of Westminster, not on progress— not yet.

Irritated by the stifling atmosphere of intrigue and unrest, Richard had set out through Reading, Oxford and the Cotswolds, northwards. He was anxious that his people should have this early opportunity to see himself and his Queen, and he was further persuaded by his wife's longing to leave the capital. He had forced himself to put aside the crippling anxiety about her advancing illness. Bravely she had greeted him when he returned from Baynards Castle. The physicians had been cautious in their prognostications but not despairing. For his crowning she had bloomed again, and now, for her dear sake, they would go north to Yorkshire where his son awaited them, that frail boy who was now England's heir and Prince of Wales.

Here at Warwick they had paused for a longer stay. The weather remained fair and the Court relaxed for the first time from the arduous duties of the past month. Beaumont's heart stirred with hope. While the Queen remained sickly Meg would not ask to leave her side and the situation had been such that he held back from seeking for permission to withdraw from active service. Now he promised himself that on their return to London, Meg would go with him to the house he had prepared for her.

He went to her now in the arbour where she was still busy gathering roses. She laughed up at him, then cried out and held a finger dark with blood. He took it, sucked out the thorn and stooped to kiss her palm.

A page called from the courtyard and he frowned. Would he never have an hour alone with Meg?

'Sir Charles, the King demands your presence.'

'Excuse me, Meg. Stay here till I come to you. I will try to be quick.'

She smiled her sympathy and he quickened his steps, smoothing down his doublet and settling his hair. One did not burst into the presence of the King in a state of disarray. The page was hard put to keep pace with him.

'The King's Grace is in his private chamber, Sir Charles, not in hall.'

Beaumont's curiosity increased. Obviously the King had work for him, and that which he did not wish to make public. At any other time he would have welcomed an opportunity for business which would take him from the scented formality of The Court Progress but now he had no wish to be parted from Meg. He compressed his lips in some doubt as to the reason for his summons.

The King was seated at his desk, Sir Francis Lovell in attendance.

'Come in, Charles. I apologise if I take you abruptly from the company of Mistress Woollat but I've need of you.'

'Your Grace has only to ask.'

Lovell went to the door and stationed the guard farther off. The King gestured for Beaumont to seat himself.

218

'Does aught keep you in England, Sir Charles?' The question caught Beaumont off balance. He made an exclamation of surprise and his blue eyes flashed and caught the grey ones of his sovereign challengingly.

'Naught, if the King's Grace orders me away, sir.' His reply was direct if somewhat frostily uttered.

Richard smiled at his coldness. 'Be not angry with me, man. Your banishment will not last long and I will not part you from your lady.'

'You wish me to take Meg?'

The King looked steadily at him. 'Aye. Will you journey to Burgundy, to my sister the Duchess?'

'I am to carry urgent dispatches?'

'You are to carry more than that.' The King gestured briefly to Lovell and he went into the adjoining bed-chamber as if obeying an unspoken order. Richard looked down at the rings on his fingers, then beckoned as Sir Francis stood in the doorway with the young Duke of York at his side. The King's voice was gentle, encouraging. 'Come to me, Dickon.'

The boy came obediently to his uncle's side. He looked from him to Beaumont. He said nothing but his eyes appealed.

Gloucester encircled him with a strong arm. 'You will do what I ask, Dickon, go with Sir Charles, obey him in all things?'

The boy swallowed but nodded. 'I would rather stay here with you, Lord Uncle—and

219

with Edward.'

'I know it.' Gloucester reached up and touched the lad's bright hair. 'But I have my reasons for asking this of you and you must trust me. I have promised you that I will send for you home the moment I can safely do so. I will keep my word. Does that content you?'

'Yes, My Lord.'

'Edward is not gravely sick. The illness will soon pass.' The physicians have assured me of a speedy recovery. Later he will join you. It was never my intention that you two should travel together. I wished you to meet Sir Charles Beaumont here in my presence and repeat your promise before me to him that you will be guided by his orders on this journey. He will act as your father. Let me see you so swear, Dickon.'

The boy turned to Beaumont and held out his hand. 'I will obey you as my uncle commands, sir.'

Beaumont bowed and the King signalled to Lovell. 'Go now into my chamber, Dickon. I will come to you soon and you must take leave of your lady aunt. Sir Francis, perhaps you would be kind enough to complete the chess game you began earlier with the Lord Richard.'

Lovell bowed and with his hand on the boy's shoulder, once more drew him into the King's bed-chamber.

Beaumont stared blankly at the King.

220

'You will have divined my fear. For the time being the boys are not safe in England—and certainly not together. Apart there is security. Who would dispose of one prince while the other lies under my protection?'

'You think him safer in Burgundy?'

'I can trust my sister. Dickon will be guided by my wishes, here or apart from me—not so the Lord Edward. The boy resents me, not unnaturally. He must remain in the Tower for the present. He is not well. What I told the boy was no lie. They will be no less happy for this separation. They have seen little of each other during the past years. The Clarence children concern me too. Margaret is no problem. Soon I will arrange a suitable marriage as I will for Edward's girls, the boy needs constant care. Later, if I feel it unsafe for him to remain here, I must make further arrangements.'

Beaumont nodded as the King paused and regarded him as if he feared contradiction.

'You heard what I said. I wish you to travel as a wealthy merchant. I have ordered your journey down to the last detail. I thought Mistress Woollat could accompany you—as your wife.' There was a slight pause before the last words and Beaumont stiffened but made no argument. 'She knows the boy and he will accept her. Have you question or objection?'

Beaumont thought quickly then shook his head. 'No, sir, none.'

'Margaret will go with you willingly?'

Beaumont's lips curved into a smile. 'I think so sir. When do you wish us to leave?'

'Tonight. No one will notice it amiss that you leave my side during this Progress. I leave soon for Leicester then north to York. By the time I reach London you could be back in England.'

Beaumont gave a sigh of open relief. He had feared permanent banishment from the King's side while the lad remained in Burgundy. He had no wish for such enforced exile.

'I have need of your services, Sir Charles. Your battle experience will prove invaluable to me.'

'It will come to that?' Beaumont's eyes gleamed in the light of the rose-coloured pane from the window.

'I believe it will come to that—but please God not until we are ready. Then I must be assured of the boy's safety. No one lord will then be able to stab me from behind so simply on the excuse that he places one or the other of Edward's sons on the Throne of England.'

'You are wise, sir.'

'Sir Piers Langham will stay by me for the present. His lady is too well known at Court to play the part I had assigned for Mistress Woollat. Despite your nearness to me during the past weeks you are not so readily known in London and you know Burgundy well. You understand the need for my choice.'

'I understand and am honoured, sir.'

222

Richard leaned forward and grasped Beaumont's hand. 'Go, speak with your lady.'

As Beaumont reached the door he said softly, 'You will be some months in Burgundy. If you had a mind to return with a wife, the Queen would be pleased to welcome her among her ladies.'

Beaumont swung round and peered across the room. The King did not drop his eyes. Beaumont read in that look a great deal that was not said. Once before Richard had revealed to him his innermost thoughts and fears. For the first time he was sure that what he must do was right—for him. The decision came suddenly without struggle and without doubt. He smiled his answer and withdrew from the King's presence.

CHAPTER TWENTY

Meg was waiting for him in the rose arbour. She stood up from her seat and started towards him as he crossed the green sward. Seeing she was alarmed by his grave expression he took her arm and led her back into the seclusion of the arbour.

'There is naught to fear, Meg.'

'But the Duchess—'

'Is well, as far as I know. She was not mentioned.' He laughed at her fear. 'Would you not have been sent for if she had taken worse?'

She nodded relieved and he waved her to the wooden seat where she'd waited for him.

'The King has work for me.'

She took it bravely. 'You must leave Court?'

'I go to Burgundy—tonight.'

'So soon?'

'That is the King's command.'

'When—' Her voice faltered. 'When do you return?'

'I know not, Meg. There is some danger in the mission. I will not keep it from you.'

His heart sank at the sick fear in her eyes as she lifted her face to his. He hated to hurt her so, but he had to be sure of her.

'God keep you.' Her whisper was soft but firm enough.

'Meg, once before I asked you to go with me on such a mission. You acted as nurse and mother then. Can I ask you to do it again?'

'You take me with you?' Her hand quivered with hope as he held it tightly in his own.

'Yes—if you are willing.'

'You know that I am.'

'Listen, sweeting, the King entrusts us with the person of the young Duke of York. He is to go to his lady aunt the Duchess of Burgundy. None must know he travels and we must be disguised, I as a merchant, wealthy enough, there is no need for penury. No one expects the King to act so. The child will not be recognised

224

and he is amenable to discipline.'

'We take only one prince?'

'Yes.' Beaumont hesitated as her dark eyes questioned him. Even yet she found it hard to trust the King's intention. 'Meg, they are safer separated one from the other, you said so yourself.'

For one moment she continued to regard him steadily as if she would ready his unspoken thoughts, then she nodded. 'Likely so. I go as your servant, is that it?'

'You go as my wife, Meg.'

She flushed and lowered her eyes. 'That seems sensible. I shall be nearer the boy if he needs comfort. If—' she broke off, rose and moved from him, 'well no matter.'

'Finish it, my Meg.'

'I was wishing to myself that you were a merchant in truth.'

'Why?'

'You would not be so far from me.'

'That still troubles you?'

'No.' Her face was turned from him and he could not read her expression. 'We have settled all that long ago. When we return—we *do* come back?'

'Yes, set your heart at rest, we return as soon as possible.'

'Then we'll go to the little house. Can we, Charles?'

'Aye, lass. The King should be back in London then. It shall be our refuge from

Court.'

'I must go and pack. Is the prince here? Can I see him?'

'Yes, later. First come here.'

She came obediently and he turned her by the shoulders to face him directly.

'Do not underestimate the dangers. Meg, they are real. If the boy *is* recognised, Richmond's agents will seek to kill him and silence us.'

'I know that.'

'And you accept your role—as my wife?'

She reached up, captured and kissed his hands, her eyes sparkling with mischief. 'Think you I cannot play the part, sir? I'm a merchant's daughter, don't forget. It will be you who could falter and spoil all by your arrogance.'

'You will remind me, Meg.'

'Do we go unescorted?'

'I shall seek to take our old friends Oates and Wilkins. They are in Sir John Gaveston's company here on duty guarding the King. I'd trust no one as I would those two.'

'Nor I.' She breathed her relief at thought of the silent Wilkins and ill-favoured, hoarse-voiced Simon Oates who'd made her comfort and safety his one concern on that journey to Kent when Beaumont had left her with the young Earl of Warwick and his sister.

'I doubt that Gaveston will deny me. I must search for him now.'

226

'You will tell him?'

He shook his head. 'Not even Gaveston. He will be content that I go on the King's business. He will not question the nature of it.' His eyes twinkled. 'Oates and Wilkins will know, of course. It might be safer and more sensible, for that matter, to leave the two of them in Burgundy with the prince.'

'The Duchess Margaret will find them strange nursemaids.'

'She will come to recognise their worth. Go now, Meg, pack what you need and wear your plainest gown and cloak.'

'Fie, sir. I'll find that less of a hardship than you will. I know you, Charles Beaumont. You are a bird who likes fine feathers.'

'You shall see the soldier in me yet, Meg, and the cheese-paring merchant, too.'

He watched her as she sped towards the castle then followed at a more sober pace to go in search of his friend, Gaveston.

Meg closed and barred the door of her room while she set about her task of packing. The Queen would be resting now and her ladies dismissed. They would lie on their beds, fanning themselves and complaining of the heat till it was time to dress for their places near their mistress. It was imperative no one intruded on her now. She packed her more extravagant possessions in one wooden box. It would travel with the rest of the royal baggage and she might yet claim it again in London. If

227

not, it would not matter. Charles would provide her with what was needful. She had little jewellery of value, one or two trinkets Charles had given her and a golden chain with a jewelled cross, a present from the Queen on the day of the coronation. She wrapped them hastily in a kerchief and hid them among her clothing. None were too garish or unsuitable for a merchant's wife. She valued these above all else she possessed, as she loved the donors. She could not leave them behind and Charles would not chide her, she felt sure.

Soberly clad in a kirtle and cloak of drab brown cloth she seated herself on her bed to await Beaumont's summons. A quiet knock brought her to her feet, biting her lip in doubt as to the wisdom of admitting any of her companions in the Queen's service.

'Mistress Woollat.'

Meg hesitated as she recognised the ringing tones of Lady Alicia Langham. She sat silent, uncertain how to answer.

'Mistress Woollat, please let me in. I come straight from the Queen.'

Meg had no choice but to open the door. She could not ignore a command from the Queen's Grace. Alicia Langham swept in with a rustle of stiff silk petticoats.

'You must come to the Queen's chamber. She sent me for you.'

'But I—'

Lady Langham laughed. 'No arguments,

228

child. You *must* obey.'

'I'm not dressed for the Queen's chamber. I—'

'So I see.' The older woman's eyebrows arched in a mystified frown. 'There is no time now. Come as you are.'

She led Meg firmly and without further protest to the Queen's chamber.

Anne was busily engaged with two maid-servants. She seemed flushed and excited but gracious as ever. They had obviously been searching through the chests of baggage for some gown the Queen needed. Meg hurried to her side at once. If she were needed to alter some gown for the feast tonight she must start immediately. What could she say to the Queen? Dare she make some excuse? Confused and worried, she was bright red with embarrassment.

'Your Grace, I thought you had been told— that is—the King has asked—'

Anne crossed to her and took her hands in her own. 'I know, Meg, you must leave me soon. All is arranged. You have no need to explain matters. Child—' she broke off to stare horrified at the drab cloak and kirtle, 'you cannot wear such garments. I had thought you might need one of mine. Thank God I had the foresight to turn out my clothing chests. Take off those things at once and come to the bath—'

'Your Grace—'

'Hurry, child. I've ordered the maids to prepare it. This gown will need adjustment but it will serve.'

Meg allowed herself to be gently pushed into the adjoining chamber where a tub-bath stood steaming with perfumed water, masked by wooden rails on which towels were stretched. A maid deftly assisted her out of her clothing and helped her into the bath. Puzzled, but helpless to resist, she allowed the girl to wash her body and hair. When she climbed out another maid towelled her hair vigorously while the first dried her and rubbed some sweet-scented salve into her body. It seemed strange that the Queen should insist on such a ritual bathing before she embarked on the journey. Meg was scrupulous about her personal cleanliness, but doubtless, since she was to wait on the prince—She gave up the effort to puzzle out the reasons. The Queen accepted her attendance, and *knew* she was careful about her appearance. Why then must she so bathe? Had Charles wished it? Her cheeks burned at the thought.

The girls giggled as they clothed her in shift and under petticoat of fine linen, garments undoubtedly borrowed from the Queen's extensive wardrobe. The Queen hastened in with Lady Langham. She surveyed Meg critically. The girl was standing bewildered and very close to tears. Anne dismissed the maids.

'Off you go, girls. I shall not need you again.

We will manage the alterations. Come here, child. Let me look at you. I think the pale yellow silk, Alicia, with the green velvet. The colour suits her brown hair. The yellow roses are best, or do you think white after all?'

Alicia Langham slipped the over-petticoat over Meg's head and spoke through a mouthful of pins. 'The yellow, I think, it compliments the gown.'

'Your Grace.' Meg whispered uncertainly. 'It is kind of you to give me a gown as a farewell gift but I must travel in plain attire. It is the King's command.'

Alicia swept her protest aside as she drew in the waist adroitly. 'Oh yes, of course. You will not travel in this, girl. Hold still or I shall prick you. Now the green velvet.' Meg stared down at the soft, green cloth which caressed her body with its richness. With her own hands the Queen brushed and combed her brown hair in shining waves on to her shoulders and took up the chaplet of yellow roses, already pressed into shape by one of her ladies.

'The thorns have been removed, Meg. There is nothing to fear. So—as I thought. The gown becomes you immensely and we are much of a size. Indeed I have not worn this gown which is just as well. Sir Charles will have no cause to complain despite our haste.'

'My Lady—'

Anne tilted the girl's chin towards her. 'Come, no tears, though in truth I know it often does happen. I felt so myself on my own wedding day and no bride loved her husband as I my Richard.' She laughed again. 'But there, all brides think so.'

'Wedding?' Meg lifted eyes over-large in a pale face. Was it so? Were Charles and she to go through this false marriage for the added safety of their mission? He had said naught to her. Her lips trembled. This would not be easy. He had no right to ask it. Surely some other contrivance would have explained their absence from Court.

The Queen was speaking briskly to Alicia. 'Stay and talk to Meg while I inform the King that all is in readiness. He will come and convey her to the chapel.'

Meg looked helplessly at the woman who had once been Charles's betrothed. Could she confide in her? Would she understand— persuade Charles that this ceremony was too much to be endured?

She was surveying her handiwork, biting her lip in doubt. 'Have you some simple trinket to wear round your throat? I have something perhaps. Stay a moment while I look—'

'Lady Langham.'

Alicia turned at the girl's heartfelt cry.

'Please, you must help me. I love him.'

'But of course you do. There is nothing to be afraid of.' The older woman's countenance lit up with mischief then real tenderness. 'You are still a maid? It is natural to have misgivings. All

232

maids do so, as the Queen said.'

'He will not wed with me. It is not fitting. I am a merchant's daughter and he—'

Alicia returned to her side, her dark eyes troubled. 'Charles loves you. Do you doubt that?'

Tearfully Meg shook her head. 'No, I believe he does. But he will not wed me. He has said so. This is but make-believe. I go as his wife—a show only.'

Alicia stopped dead before and looked deep into her tear-filled eyes. 'The priest waits in the private chapel. He—'

'I see the bride is ready.'

Alicia turned as the King stood smiling in the doorway, his hand outstretched to take that of Meg.

'My Lord.' Meg swept into a deep curtsey. Her eyes continued to plead with Alicia for guidance.

Alicia looked from her to the King. She hesitated, gave a sudden nervous cough as if suppressing some word of protest then curtseyed too and drew Meg firmly towards her sovereign.

'Surely, sir. As you see, she looks well.'

The King took Meg's cold hand into his grasp and patted it encouragingly.

'Sir Charles will have no cause for complaint despite the hastiness of the preparations. Come, my child, let us go. The priest is waiting.'

Meg allowed herself to be led, but outside the chapel door she pulled back and whispered, 'My Lord, I must talk with Sir Charles before—'

'This is no time for faint-heartedness, Meg.' The King's voice betrayed amusement. 'Soon, you'll have all night to speak with Sir Charles if you'll want to talk then, that is.' He chuckled then as he saw she was closer to tears than he could have imagined. He turned to her and looked into her eyes, 'What is it, Meg?'

'Must I—must I do this?'

He frowned, perplexed. 'Nay, child, no one forces you to this. I was told it was your wish.' He stared over her bent head and thought he caught the sound of a faint sob, but for the moment her face was hidden from him.

Hearing footsteps Beaumont had come impatiently to the door of the chapel. He caught his breath as Meg's loveliness, her nut-brown hair denoting her virgin state, loose about her shoulders. He offered a silent prayer of gratitude to God that he had not taken her, that she was unspoilt, coming to him now, as he had dreamed his bride would, untouched and more than a whit afraid. There had been so many instances when he could have possessed her and had held back from the act. In his cold bed, he had often times regretted his folly, yet now he knew his forbearance had been planned from the beginning. The first time in 'The Golden Cockerel' she had offered herself. It would have then been a simple matter to have taken her body as payment for his protection of her. He had refused then, recognising her as the child she was, then later, when he knew her as true woman, he had delayed. He caught the King's eyes, puzzled. Richard raised his shoulders in a faint shrug of helplessness.

Beaumont came quickly to their side. 'What ails you, Meg? We keep the priest waiting. Have you no wish to be my wife?'

Hot colour flamed her cheeks. 'You shame me, sir. You know how it is with me, has ever been. But this—this mock ceremony. It hurts me.'

Understanding flashed through his being. The glitter faded from those steely blue eyes. He bent and took both her hands. 'Meg, you wrong me. This is no mockery. Here in the chapel the Queen's confessor will wed us, before we go on the King's business.'

'You mean it—this is what you wish? You are sure?'

'Very sure, Meg. Looking at you now, I have never been surer.'

'But my dower—you said—'

'Concern yourself not about your dower, Mistress Woollat. That shall be attended to, I assure you.' The King's tone was suave. Even now he stood courteously waiting, during their exchange, betraying no hint of the impatience he might well have been feeling.

Beaumont looked up at the King's raised

brow. He was conscious that Meg was now closer than ever to tears. He must check them at all costs. He recalled her to her duty.

'I must go back to the priest. You are ready?'

She nodded once, her lip trembling, then he left her and the King took up her hand again to lead her into the chapel.

That night while she was attended by Lady Langham and two of the Queen's ladies, she heard hardly one word of their giggling banter. The King had refused to hear of their journeying tonight after all. 'One night cannot delay you over long,' he had said smiling. 'I will not force Sir Charles and Lady Beaumont to spend their wedding night between the damp sheets of some tavern room. Besides, I will not forgo the pleasure of seeing you bedded.' So it would be tomorrow at first light that they would set out for the coast with the younger prince.

Alicia Langham shooed the other women away and came to the side of the wide bed where Meg sat alone and forlorn, her fingers clutching the linen sheets high round her shoulders.

'One word of advice,' the older woman said briskly. 'Charles is but a man. Treat him so. Let him hear no nonsense about your merchant father. He has chosen you, wed you. Be sure he loves you well. I know Charles Beaumont. Once I thought I might be the virgin bride awaiting him in that bed.' She laughed, a joyous sound. 'I would not have been so unwilling either—until I loved my Piers. He is a yeoman's son and I was ward to Warwick the Kingmaker. I had no regrets at my choice, not then—or since. See that Charles has none. It will be for you to ensure that. he is proud, ambitious—a bad enemy and if I am any judge a lover to be coveted.' She bent closer and kissed the girl's forehead. Just once for a moment Meg clung to her.

'Did he love you, truly?'

'No, child. Charles loved nothing but power—until he looked on you. He has opened his heart to me. I know. Do not be afraid that this match will ill befit him. The King will see he loses not by it. Richard of England knows the worth of his friends.' Her face clouded as she said hurriedly, 'I would God he knew his enemies as well.'

When Lady Langham left her, Meg lay back thoughtful. The tension had gone from her at Alicia's homily. She was no longer afraid, or ashamed, not even when the men brought Charles to her bed, and the chamber rang with their lewd, wine-drenched admonitions. The King at length ordered them firmly back to the hall below, closing the door with his own hands.

The scent of the lavender and crushed herb with which the bridal bed had been strewn came to her nostrils as Charles enfolded her in his arms. She forgot about the Court, the

237

prince, tomorrow's mission—all but the sweetness of giving herself to the man who had been her whole life since that first night when he'd stood in the doorway of 'The Crossed Keys', the man whom the Queen's Confessor had joined to her in a union blessed by the Holy Church.

We hope you have enjoyed this Large Print book. Other Chivers Press or G.K. Hall Large Print books are available at your library or directly from the publishers. For more information about current and forthcoming titles, please call or write, without obligation, to:

Chivers Press Limited
Windsor Bridge Road
Bath BA2 3AX
England
Tel. (01225) 335336

OR
G.K. Hall
P.O. Box 159
Thorndike, ME 04986
USA
Tel. (800) 223–6121
(207) 948–2962
(in Maine and Canada, call collect)

All our Large Print titles are designed for easy reading, and all our books are made to last.